PENUMBRA

The Short Stories and Poems of

Conrad Richard Edward Kolbe

With Selections by

Katherine Brown, Eunice Ross, and Conrad Richard Kolbe, Jr.

Compiled by Mary Albanese

Conrad Richard Edward Kolbe
1916

PENUMBRA

The Short Stories and Poems of

Conrad Richard Edward Kolbe

With Selections by

Katherine Brown, Eunice Ross, and Conrad Richard Kolbe, Jr.

Compiled by Mary Albanese

PENUMBRA

Published by Oxshott Press

Edited by Mary Albanese
www.MaryAlbanese.com

First printed in 1988
2nd Edition Copyright © 2012 by Mary Albanese

ISBN 978-0-9568322-2-1

PENUMBRA

for our family

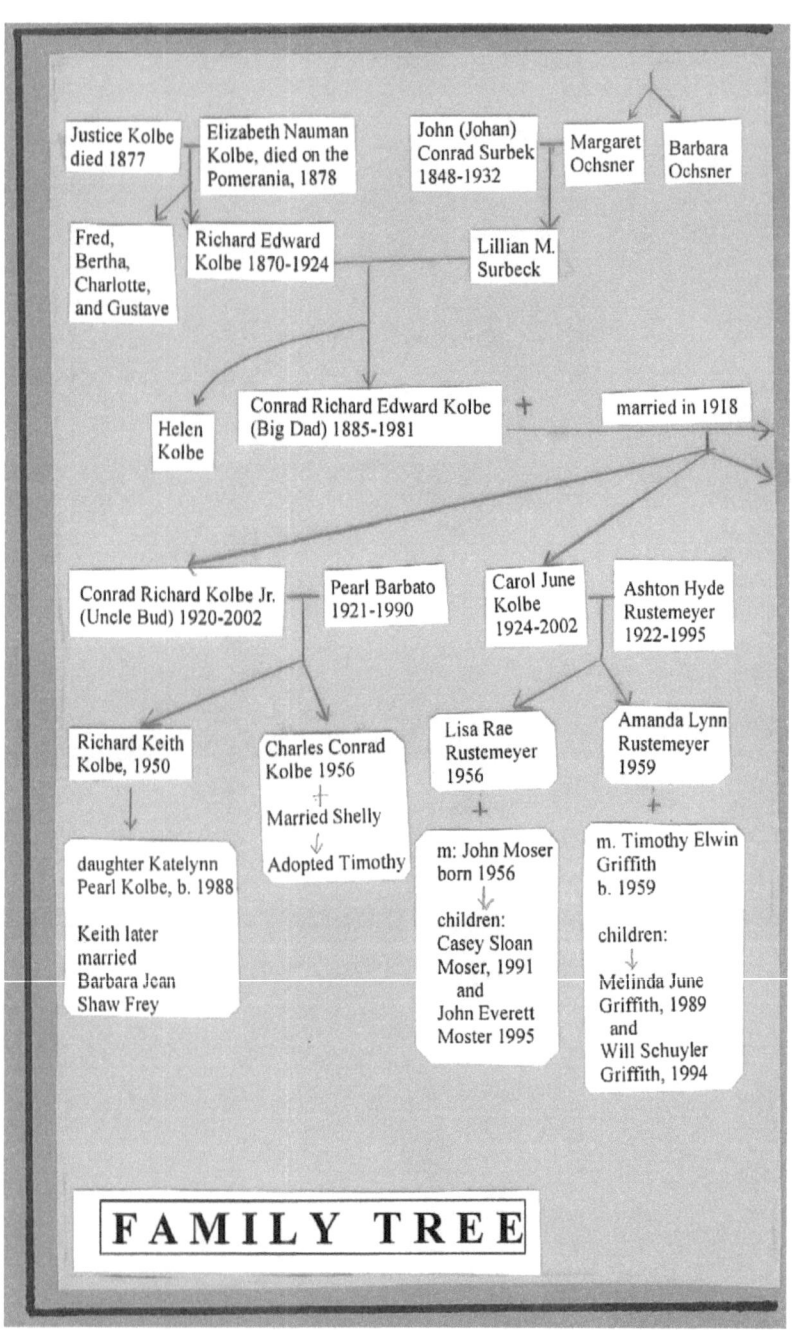

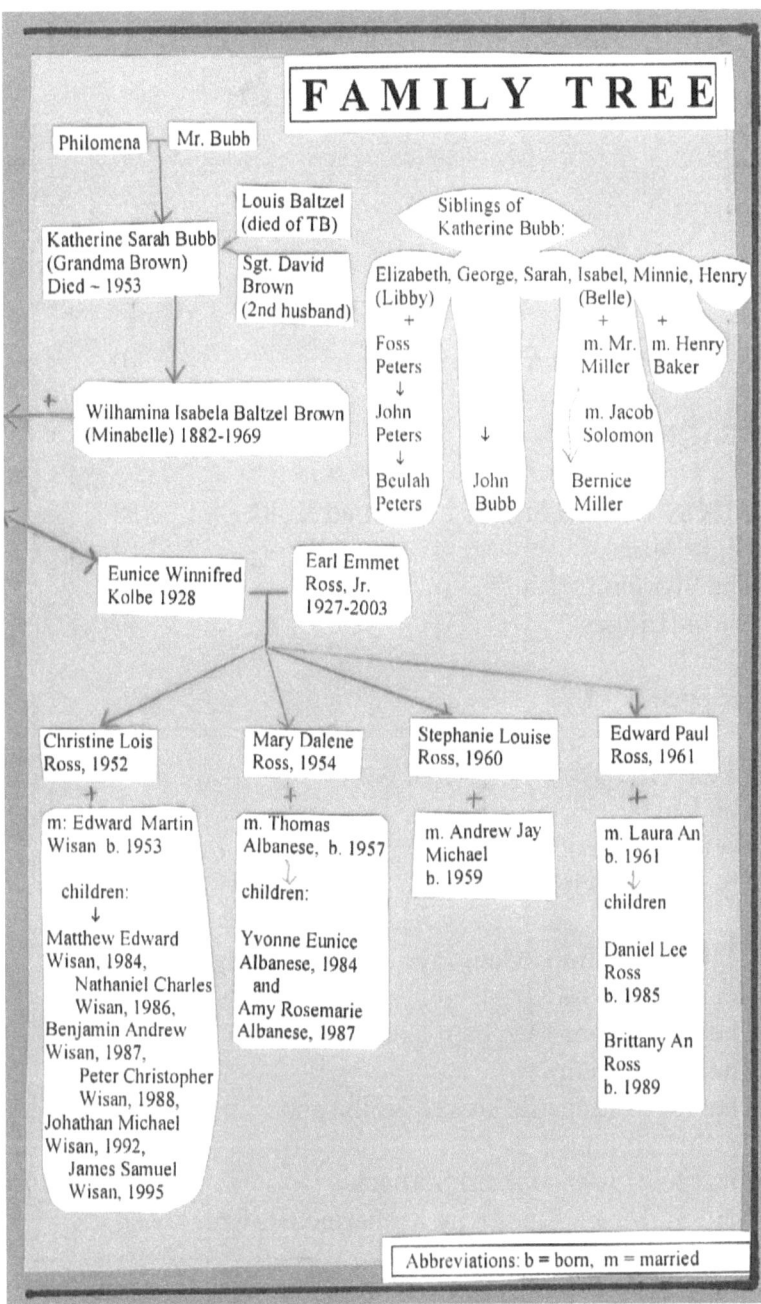

FAMILY TREE

Philomena — Mr. Bubb

Louis Baltzel (died of TB)

Katherine Sarah Bubb (Grandma Brown) Died ~ 1953

Sgt. David Brown (2nd husband)

Siblings of Katherine Bubb:

Elizabeth, George, Sarah, Isabel, Minnie, Henry (Libby) (Belle) + + + Foss m. Mr. m. Henry Peters Miller Baker ↓ John m. Jacob Peters ↓ Solomon ↓ Beulah John Bernice Peters Bubb Miller

Wilhamina Isabela Baltzel Brown (Minabelle) 1882-1969

Eunice Winnifred Kolbe 1928

Earl Emmet Ross, Jr. 1927-2003

Christine Lois Ross, 1952
+
m: Edward Martin Wisan b. 1953

children:
↓
Matthew Edward Wisan, 1984,
  Nathaniel Charles Wisan, 1986,
Benjamin Andrew Wisan, 1987,
  Peter Christopher Wisan, 1988,
Johathan Michael Wisan, 1992,
  James Samuel Wisan, 1995

Mary Dalene Ross, 1954
+
m. Thomas Albanese, b. 1957
↓
children:

Yvonne Eunice Albanese, 1984 and Amy Rosemarie Albanese, 1987

Stephanie Louise Ross, 1960
+
m. Andrew Jay Michael b. 1959

Edward Paul Ross, 1961
+
m. Laura An b. 1961
↓
children

Daniel Lee Ross b. 1985

Brittany An Ross b. 1989

Abbreviations: b = born, m = married

CONTENTS

ILLUSTRATIONS

PREFACE

by

Mary Albanese

T his volume contains five short stories and three poems written by Conrad Richard Edward Kolbe around 1926. Also contained is a section of poems written by his mother-in-law, the award-winning poetess Katherine Sarah Baltzel Brown, as well as selected poems by Conrad's son, Conrad Richard Kolbe, Jr. (Uncle Bud). In addition, included is a section of family memories and history by Eunice Kolbe Ross.

Conrad Richard Edward Kolbe was born on September 21, 1885 in Syracuse, New York and lived there all his life. Conrad Kolbe had a very sensitive and poetic nature that is clearly evident in these works. He was once asked what was his favorite color. "Green," he answered. He was asked if that was because green was the color of money. "No," he replied, "because green is the color of life."

He also loved history and was very proud that his family was instrumental in much of Syracuse's early history. His father, Richard Kolbe, owned the first foreign automobile and the first automobile distributorship in Syracuse (see Section 3). When Conrad was four years old, his uncle Gustave A. Kolbe became the first soldier killed in the Spanish American War (see figure 3-2.) Conrad's maternal grandfather, John Conrad Surbeck, was a soldier in the Civil War and was assigned as the body guard for General Custer (figure 3-4.). John Surbeck survived the Civil War and afterwards, returned to Syracuse and ran a prosperous feed mill on the Erie Canal. Young Conrad once travelled to Gettysburg with his grandfather John Surbeck and there studied the great battles of the Civil War. Listening intently as his grandfather relived his experiences of the war, Conrad was greatly impressed and took numerous photographs as his grandfather talked. Later, he presented grandfather Surbeck with a photo album of the memorable trip.

Conrad dearly wanted to attend college. This fact disappointed his grandfather, John Surbeck, who wanted Conrad to join him at the feed mill instead. Surbeck was so disappointed that he refused to help pay for Conrad's college education.

Conrad applied for a scholarship at Syracuse University as he could not attend college without one. He did not get a scholarship at first but was placed at the top of a waiting list. That summer, one young man declined his position and scholarship and it was offered to Conrad.

Conrad graduated from Syracuse University and was very proud of his education. One of his professors had a saying that Conrad liked to quote: "Even if I couldn't use my college education to get a fine job, even if the only job I could get was to drive a trash cart pulled by a donkey, I would still want the education so I could put as much distance between me and that donkey as possible."

As a young man, Conrad attended Westminster Presbyterian Church (originally called First Ward Presbyterian Church) on Syracuse's North Side. In a "Christian Endeavors" youth group, he met 'Minabelle' (Wilhamina Isabella) Baltzel Brown. They were married in the church on June 30, 1918. Minabelle, named after two aunts Minnie and Belle, was the daughter of Katherine Sarah Bubb and Louis Baltzel. Minabelle's father Louis died quite young, and her mother Katherine went on to marry Sergeant

David Brown, who helped raise Minabelle and became her beloved step-father.

Minabelle's mother Katherine eventually become a poet of some note. For more on her life and her poetry, see sections three and four. Katherine's formal education had been truncated at an early age, and it really amazed Big Dad (and probably drove him a little crazy) that she had won a rather prestigious poetry award despite not having finished high school.

Conrad and Minabelle were married over 50 years and lived in their house at 3412 James Street for almost all of their married lives. It was in that house (see section five) that they raised their family, and there that Conrad wrote the stories in this collection. Together, Conrad and Minabelle had three children: Conrad Richard Kolbe, Jr., Carol June Kolbe, and Eunice Winnifred Kolbe.

Eunice recalls that the Westminster Presbyterian Church where Conrad and Minabelle had met ended up playing a very big role in their lives. Throughout the years not only were many of the marriages and baptisms held there but during the depression, the church provided the hub of the family's social life and entertainment by hosting plays, dinners, and bazaars.

As the family expanded Conrad and Minabelle had eight grandchildren who were born (in chronological order): Richard Keith Kolbe, Christine Lois Ross, Mary Dalene Ross, Lisa Rae Rustemeyer, Charles Conrad Kolbe, Amanda Lynn Rustemeyer, Stephanie Louise Ross, and Edward Paul Ross.

Conrad and Minabelle held their 50th anniversary party in 1968. It was quite a joyful celebration. A year later, Minabelle died in 1969. Conrad died eleven years later in 1981, survived by his sister Helen, who had become Mrs. Helen Botsford of Springfield, New York.

His family was very dear to Conrad. At one time Big Dad (as he was known to many of us) told me that he never knew what his real purpose in life was until he had grandchildren. He said, "Now I know why I was born."

This volume contains his original works, unchanged. Some of the stories in this collection are dated 1926. The rest were probably written about that time. Also included are appendices on the family history as well as the history of his former house, the brick structure and Syracuse landmark at 3412 James Street, Syracuse, New York.

Ed Ross collected and saved Big Dad's poems and short stories for all of us to share. In fact, it was Ed's idea to incorporate the works into a book. He also supplied the blueprints of the house plans for the stately brick home at 3412 James Street where so many treasured family memories were made. Eunice Kolbe (Ross) provided much of the background history, and Christine Ross (Wisan) supplied many of the photos and information on the family history. I am not sure how I acquired the other photographs but I believe I can thank Keith Kolbe for them.

A previous version of this book was printed in 1988 as a limited edition for Conrad's beloved family members, including children and grandchildren. Since then a number of great-grandchildren have been added to the family. With the advent of publish-on-demand printing, this current edition is being produced so that his work will be available via searches for anyone interested in the material. In this way I am seeking to add his words and works to the collective text of mankind, which I think he would have enjoyed.

The title PENUMBRA comes from Conrad himself as it was the original title of the short story he later renamed "Burnt Bridges."

I have enjoyed putting this little volume together. In these works, I have found a facet of Conrad Kolbe that I hadn't seen before. This is the work of a young man who, as he himself explains to a prospective editor in 1926, is "afflicted with a perennial urge to write but lack... almost everything except the bare determination to write." In these pages you will meet the dashing Captain Ted Hardy and the lovely and courageous Beatrice in the science fiction thriller "The Scorpion's Tail" as they fight the evil Marmaduke of Eurasia and his sinister invasion of America with the dreaded "tetra lither maxinol pellicules." Upon reading this story, written sometime around 1926, I couldn't help but notice that the bad guy (the evil Marmaduke of Eurasia with his black whiskers) reminds me of Hitler. In the story, this villain who loves "pomp and ceremony" takes over Europe and Asia, then storms the US and plans to let only one person in five live because he considers the rest to be genetically inferior. How prophetic that the story predicts such an outrageous villain, then ends the war with the west developing a weapon of mass destruction (not an atom bomb but a "pellicule" bomb and ray gun contraption) that descends on the enemy from an "aeroplane" and wipes out great chunks of people, structures, and land, forcing the enemy to surrender.

In the story "Stripped" you will meet Hugh McDonald who is held at gun point by a young woman and is ordered to remove his clothing. This story with its twist ending is the only one of the collection that Conrad wrote using a pseudonym, that of Richard Edward. In another tale, two young lovers become engaged after a rousing game of modified deck tennis on a private yacht, which reminds me of Conrad and Minabelle's courtship, much of which was done on the tennis courts. And in the poem "Death of a Child" you can clearly feel young Conrad's pain upon the loss of his infant daughter.

Though the works are stylized in the writing conventions of the time, the stories are highly imaginative with an undeniable flair for adventure. The works display a wonderful sense of humor that is unmistakably Big Dad, and there is usually a jolly good ending for the deserving heroes and heroines.

Figure 1. Conrad and Minabelle Kolbe around 1920 at Schiller Park Tennis Courts, Syracuse, N.Y.

I hope this collection gives you some pleasurable, reflective moments. Big Dad always wanted his writings to be published and appreciated, and I am delighted to be able to do that for him. In a cover letter to a prospective publisher he once wrote, "Here's just to luck!" I would like to offer another toast. Here's to you, Big Dad. We miss you.

SECTION 1

The Short Stories of Conrad Richard Kolbe (Big Dad)

NIGHT MARE

R ichard Harrison Eustis awoke with a quiver of fear.

His heart was thumping heavily against his ribs. If his tongue, his throat, had not been so unspeakably dry, he would have believed that his own scream had awakened him.

"This comes of eating lobster too late at night," he chided himself. Despite his efforts to compose himself for sleep, the sharp, suffocating detail of his dream persisted in his mind. He had, it appeared, been fishing a dark river, and suddenly, in the unaccountable way of dreams, he held only a short length of line tied at each end with a hook, yet both hooks entered into the bait.

"Fish," demanded an inner voice of authority as he had cast. Almost immediately had come the strike. Before he could see his catch, the voice of authority commanded, "Go home."

His wife, he realized in his dream, was in dire need of his assistance. This seemed very strange because soon she would have put herself beyond the reach of whatever protection their present relationship implied. But in the cellar of his own house he sought her, the fish line now become a club. Without warning, the huge shadowy form of a woman leaped toward him, and he, grown paralyzed in arms and legs, stood helpless. Then, mercifully, he had awakened.

He turned his hot pillow to no avail. Sleep was not in him. Why should he be so disturbed by a dream about a wife who was ready to drop him for no better reason, actually, than that he had become dull and inattentive. How ironically she would laugh if she caught him peering at her in the dark, showing concern for her safety! Yet if he were to sleep again this night, he must first see her.

Noiselessly, he crept across the hallway to where a door, left open for a better circulation of air, gave into her bedroom. The orderly appearance of the room quieted his vague fears. In the dim light from outside, his wife's form lay where it should be in the bed. He turned away with a welcome sense of relief. At that instant, the shadowy figure of a woman, larger in form than his wife, appeared in the open doorway and he, stunned by her unexpected apparition, let her pass.

"Who are you?" he demanded in a thick whisper.

The woman screamed and darted toward the stairs leading to the servants' quarters. The sound of choked sobbing floated down to him. He would have followed but a queer noise in his wife's bedroom distracted his attention. Darkly, against the dim outline of a window, loomed a figure, a figure in a slouch hat, which moved about in nervous passes. Eustis stepped forward and stumbled over a fragile chair.

"Stop where y'are or I'll drop ya, see. Now get out of here," snarled the dark figure ominously.

Richard Harrison Eustis, thus ordered out of his wife's bedroom, felt a surge of passionate rage sweep over him. He groped for the chair at his feet, caught it up, and lunged in the direction of the intruder. A crash of wood against wood came with a jarring impact. The bark of a gun, the flash of searing fire meant little to Eustis in his violent, his hysterical anger, save that it revealed the direction in which he must strike again. The next blow found its human target, there was a dull, sickening thud and the man went down with a sharp outcry.

Eustis unsteadily turned on the lights. His wife lay motionless across the bed, her face wrapped in a broad bandage. This he removed with feverish fingers, for the telltale odor of chloroform had become heavy in the room. Presently, after he had had time to call and doctor and the police, his wife stirred and opened her eyes wide upon his face.

"Richard, I'm so glad you got here. When I recognized Marthe, the new maid, I am sure that fellow who was with her meant to kill me."

"Never mind now, Ellen. I've settled for him, I guess. With your permission, I'll stay on a while," he ventured stiffly.

Ellen lay very still and wax-like, but her eyes danced like luminous star points. Combined with the dead odor of chloroform in the room, was a faint scent de hyacinth, reminiscent of the time, not so many years back, when Ellen was a bright flame and he the oil, eager to be burnt. Her voice, when she spoke, came as from a great distance.

"They were going to tie this on you, make it appear as if you had killed me. Of course, the servants know I was planning a divorce, and with that woman, Marthe, to testify against you they might have made a case. I was awfully sorry for you."

"You thought of *me* when they were killing *you*!" Eustis was frankly incredulous.

"The point is," said Ellen dreamily, "you came. Honestly, I haven't thought of you in any decent way for a long time, but tonight, even before they came, I sort of wanted to call it off. Just the right word of encouragement from you, Richard, but you never were strong in words, were you?"

Richard Eustis searched under the dainty covers for the face that was elusively withheld. He remembered this as an old trick of Ellen's. Her lips turned, suddenly, squarely to his own. There were interrupted almost at once by the insistent ringing of the doorbell, the heavy tread of men on the stair.

THE SCORPION'S TAIL

Captain Ted Hardy, flying coast patrol on the morning of

May 15, 1998 felt the penetrating chill of gloom which hung, heavy-lidded, over the eastern seaboard. Ordinary business seemed to have been dropped, everywhere were little knots of people, talking excitedly, and whose upturned white faces were scarcely reassured by the red hawk emblem on Ted's Amphibian.

High over the eastern horizon or Washington in mysterious letters of smoke which changed to a green fire at dusk, hung the ultimatum of the Grand Marmaduke of Eurasia, that merciless potentate who had risen from obscurity in Moslem India to become the commanding figure in all the Eastern Hemisphere. The actual fact of the sky writing was of secondary importance, for his secret agents might be anywhere, but what really did matter was the demand to the western continents for an instant, an abject surrender. The ultimatum included the Marmaduke's customary form of decimation then practiced in Eurasia, whereby all who fell below a certain standard would be speedily put out of the way. Second, children would be sent to qualified schools and any who failed the tests would conveniently "die of a fever." Third, and most galling to the Western spirit, a selected group of women, headed by the President's daughter, were required to be turned over to the

Marmaduke and his regents for the purpose of bearing their children.

Concurrently with the delivery of the ultimatum at Washington in the north, and at La Capitola in the Latin south, the vast armada of the Marmaduke had swung out into the Atlantic on its fatal mission. There would be three days of grace.

The televisor in Ted Hardy's plane had reflected the embarking of the uncountable flotilla, gleaming ships stamped out of an un-corrosive alloy. Some five hundred million other eyes had seen the endless columns of warriors, in their red and white uniforms as they stood in formation on the enemy decks. The sending of the host of soldiers, Ted realized, was a gesture of power really unnecessary on the part of the Eastern Overlord, save that it indulged his natural love of pomp and ceremony. In January, he had announced that his chemists had evolved a secret element, so potent in effect that one pellicule, fired from a draft gun, could destroy all life within the radius of fifteen miles. The draft guns had also been so perfect that they could propel large pellicules for the incredible distance of one hundred miles before dropping their deadly charges.

Thus would the defences of the American continents be silenced before the sting of their hitherto effective long range guns could be felt.

At twenty minutes after ten, Ted's radio indicator flashed red giving him pause in his seaward observations to listen to the voice from headquarters. "Report at once at Hanger A," was the curt order.

He avoided the region where the smoky warning hung in the sky as he would a plague, but within fifteen minutes he was descending into the broad and all but deserted landing field. Two mechanics dashed forward and applied themselves vigorously with the plane while a large car, appearing as if from nowhere, sped toward him and paused, waiting. On the door was the great eagle of the United States, the President's own car.

"The White House?" asked Ted in astonishment. The chauffeur, who looked distinguished enough to be an assistant secretary of aviation, nodded gravely. He devoted his entire attention to what was developing into an exceedingly rapid trip through the historic streets of the dignified capital. Ted refrained from further questions. He assumed that the matter was important and that he would soon learn whatever details were intended for him.

Without ceremony, Ted was conducted to a part of the White House which he recognized at once as reserved for the private use of the President and his family. President Fairkind himself greeted Ted with a warm handshake and then presented him to the girl whose beauty and attainments, more than any other circumstance, had aroused the Marmaduke's desire.

"Young man," said the President, while a kindly smile temporarily replaced his harassed look. "I hear you are to be trusted. Is that true?"

"If you are asking my opinion," answered Ted, "I am."

"Good," said Christopher Fairkind. "I believe you. I shall place under your protection, my most important possession and, some have been gracious enough to say, one of the greatest of the country. My daughter. At any rate, she has come to represent all American womanhood, for what happens to her will largely determine the fate of all the rest. Your business, young man, will be to fly to a spot on a map which I shall give you, to destroy the map as soon as you have landed and to tell no one what has taken place. Above all, be sure to bring the plane back with you, and alone."

"Righto." Ted saluted.

"But, father, they will not destroy Washington while I remain." She couldn't quite suppress a certain quivering of her lips.

Christopher Fairkind quelled his daughter's outburst with a look and a wave of his hand, the last flare-up of an argument worn threadbare. Ted wasn't sorry to find that a Class A young woman could pack a considerable degree of spunk.

"They would hardly destroy the capital, if they don't really know where you are. You would certainly be captured here, and you know what that means."

"This," said Beatrice, as she produced a small vial plainly marked with a lurid warning.

Her eyes met Ted's. He would have sworn that they were asking him, "Wouldn't *you* be sorry?" The vague horror of the fast approaching catastrophe suddenly became crystallized for Ted by the fate which was hanging over the girl who seemed so young and so full of the zest for life. He glanced quizzically at the President and saw that his head was bowed, the harassed lines graven deeply into his face.

"It is time," said the President quickly. "You must go." Ted turned away, his eyes swimming, as he embraced his daughter affectionately.

Beatrice Fairkind left the White House dressed as a member of the coast guard. The tell-tale lines of her sex were concealed under a loose fitting storm ulster. At the steps, a closed car waited with the same distinguished chauffeur at the wheel. Beatrice hastened within and, smiling at his indecision, motioned Ted to follow. Alone with the young woman, over whom the world was about to go into desperate grips, Ted felt a bit embarrassed, especially when he felt her shoulder against his as if mutely pleading for the protection his sex still signified. What a tragic situation this was for the girl who had become another, and even greater Helen. As if in answer to his thoughts, he could feel a quiver run through her body.

"The Marmaduke is a beast," said Beatrice. "He has a dark face which is full of negroid whiskers. DO you think if I give myself up to him, he would spare the country?"

"They say he will spare only one out of five. The best according to his standards. But many of these would rather die than consent to his conditions of life."

"War is a murderous thing," said Beatrice gravely. "Fifty years ago, in 1948, they said it would be like a scorpion with a stinger in its tail which had become so vindictive and so deadly that it must eventually turn back and slay itself. How much better, in times like these, to be a man. To be able to fight!"

"The fighting spirit of the people seems paralyzed by the suddenness of the attack. What can be done in two more days against such weapons?"

"We could, at least, die in the attempt!" As Ted looked into the blazing fury of her eyes, he felt an almost insane desire to lay down and die if only she might live. He circled her with a protecting arm when, conscious of his error, he awaited her reproach. Instead, she drew his face down to her own and looked at him intently. "You will fight, won't you?"

"To the end, of course."

Surprisingly, she kissed him. Ted couldn't be sure whether the kiss was a symbol intended for the fighting manhood of America, or whether the larger share was really meant for him. He was, he decided, a bit presumptuous, but he preferred his own opinion.

They had reached the aviation field, a small one well across the Virginia state line on the road to Alexandria. Ted saw that some mechanics were warming up the motor in a beautiful new plane.

What's her ceiling?" he asked curiously.

A mechanic turned to grin. "Don't know, boss. Guess she's never been up."

Ted grimaced. "Well, I'll let you know when I get back, if I do."

"We're go'nta expect you, captain."

Ted gave her the gun and taxied out to the open field. The plane was almost incredibly responsive to his lightest pull on the stick, and he had scarcely lifted her over the outer rim of the trees when he began to feel that secret attachment which a good pilot experiences for a superior piece of mechanism.

His enthusiasm was suddenly checked with an abruptness which made him reel. Concealed by a light screen of trees, a man was deliberately shooting at them with a craftily hidden machine gun. Ted grimly faced ahead on the outside chance that, in spite of their low elevation, they might get past. He became aware that the slim figure of his companion was in a state of great animation. Poor kid, it might as well be now. Yet she seemed to know what she was about, pressing buttons on a trick battery that Ted had hardly time to be curious about and presently she pulled out a glass nozzle attached to a long tube, which she pointed at the man. As they passed over him, a look of pained surprise appeared in his face. Ted had the odd notion that he had turned black. Beatrice betrayed so great a degree of excitement that Ted decided to strap her to the seat as soon as they attained sufficient elevation.

When they had gone up to a very great altitude, Beatrice removed her helmet, so that her hair, soft and silky, fluffed about her head like a brown cocoon. A deep flush still reddened her cheek, and her eyes, darkly blue, were smoky with emotion.

"I've killed my first man," she exclaimed through taut lips.

"What is that jack-box?" Ted glanced in the direction of a strange assortment of coils, wires and bottled chemicals.

Beatrice, bent on an affair of her own, ignored his question.

"Would you break your promise to the President if there was a chance of turning the Marmaduke's ships, perhaps of destroying them?"

"Do I look like a fellow who would forget what he said?"

"You are evading my question. It's a matter of stakes. If you could save western society from the unspeakable Marmaduke, would you forget it?"

"You are asking me a tough question."

"I mean -- would you?"

"No."

"Please think it over for a minute," she pleaded. "If, by breaking your promise, you would save a hundred million lives, and prevent the rest from suffering under that horrible cult of Ossidian, would you do it? Not alone -- you and I together."

"No."

A look of utter exasperation appeared in Beatrice's face. "You are a great fool, and so have I been. You are the world's worst coward and generations of children in classrooms will learn your name with reproach along with that of Benedict Arnold. Because you had the chance to turn the Marmaduke and you weren't big enough to take it. And to think that I asked -- but never mind." She collapsed into a tense, a violent silence.

They had left the cities and scattered settlements of the valley behind them for the tapestried woodlands which were the blue Alleghenies. It was increasingly evident to Ted that Beatrice was bitterly resenting the widening progress of their flight. Thin drops of blood had broken through the tender skin of her lips where she had bitten them and when she spoke, it was in the far-away voice of an ambitious child who had been painfully rebuffed.

"I suppose you think that I was only talking nonsense when I said that you and I might stop the battleships. Maybe it was. Perhaps what I shall tell you now will be surprising. Promise, first, that you will never say a word to anyone?"

"Of course," replied Ted amiably. He hadn't found it easy to deny her wish.

"You saw that man turn black, just beyond the landing field. I stung him."

"You what?"

"Stung him. It's a magnetic ray that is shot from a bed of chemicals, with any point on the earth as a focus. All living matter in the path of the ray is blackened to a crisp."

"Where did you get that idea?" Ted shuddered, despite his military training.

"In a chemistry class. It developed from an accident that happened when I was mixing some elements which I had no right to be using. Really, I wouldn't dare tell you how stupid I am in a laboratory. My poor professor nearly was killed."

"But why hasn't that thing been perfected? Do you suppose it would counteract their tetra litho maxinol pellicles?"

"Ted!" Her eyes were so beautiful and troubled and full of tears that he wanted to give in to the request he knew was coming. "Why couldn't we go out there and find out?"

"No. Don't ask that again. What could we do against a million men? Even if we burned up a thousand or so, their aeroplanes would get us."

"You don't understand. If we could explode one of those pellicules that they claim are so deadly, wouldn't we destroy their entire fleet?"

"Do you think your magnetic ray could do that?"

"Well, not positively. But couldn't a well-aimed pistol shot do that much?"

"Good Lord, I never thought of that. Yet what would happen to us?"

"Oh, why should that matter? They tell me that I am the cause of the Marmaduke's invasion, and I am determined that he shall never take me alive. Since my life is in forfeit anyway, there is everything to gain. It's not even necessary that you should go."

The girl's spirits were so obviously sunk, that Ted let go of the stick just long enough to pat her reassuringly.

"Look out!" she exclaimed. "You are losing elevation when you should be climbing. Do you want to hit that mountain?"

"Don't be like that," returned Ted, moodily. He missed the mountain by a bare fifty feet.

Beatrice curled up remotely at the farther side of the seat and turned her back to him with more than necessary emphasis. "You had better give me the stick," she said, mercilessly.

They were climbing pretty steadily now. According to Ted's calculations, they had about reached their destination. He hated to leave Beatrice in her uncertain temper, but his orders were not to be mistaken.

"If you should need protection," Beatrice told him stiffly at parting, "you can open the projector by turning on this switch. All the other adjustments are made. If you value your life, don't let the ray touch you or any part of the ship. And keep it down. It's not effective unless it comes to focus on the earth."

Dark eyes, smoky with their suppressed eagerness, swam before Ted as he sped back to Washington. Poor kid. After all, why couldn't they have gone on this last mad adventure together? She would die anyway, because that was better than to have the Marmaduke take her alive. His impatience with himself increased until he could stand his own thoughts no longer, and he fumbled with the deadly projector to escape them. He sighted down the glass funnel at a lake, a barn, a haystack. Curious, he turned on the switch. The odor of hot sulphur puckered his nostrils while the haystack below burst into flames.

Hastily, he threw off the switch. A strange sense of power quickened his blood, the image of Beatrice came before him, her kiss, which he realized now was meant as the seal to an unspoken covenant between them. He gripped the stick tightly in desperate resolution.

Ted sighted the enemy armada between three hundred and two hundred miles out, early in the morning of the last day of grace. Far below him, the decks were in a state of orderly commotion with platoons of soldiers executing military drills, while the fleet itself appeared to be separating into smaller divisions. For a brief moment, he realized how absurd was his position, one man pitted against a million, with a weapon, the effectiveness of which was still to be proven. If the fleet below him had a similar defence, his mission was ended before it had begun. These thoughts didn't interfere with his purpose; in fact, he had ceased to regard himself as a person but rather as an instrument of destruction poised for its final thrust at the target.

A flight of aeroplanes rose like giant flying fish from their mother ship, showing that he had been sighted. Quickly he dialed the long distance enunciator and addressed himself directly to Kurstand Baldassar, reputed to be chief in command.

"Grand Marshall Baldassar, recall your aeroplanes, or I shall burn them down. Make no further hostile move or your fleet will be immediately destroyed. Hold all vessels close for orders. If you disobey you will be blown out of the water within a minute."

At once, all was confusion on the decks below. No doubt, thousands of faces were turned upward wondering at the strange voice which menaced them from above. The aeroplanes, beyond recall, came on. Ted directed his projector at the point where they would pass beyond the line of the battleships, and as they reached this spot, he saw them fall like signed moths into the ocean. A new sense of power surged through him as he realized that perhaps the destiny of his people lay in his hands as well as the lives of a million enemy soldiers and sailors. He had but to explode one pellicule and the entire fleet would be instantly annihilated. How stupid of their Grand Marshall to overlook so essential a detail.

He focused his televisor on the largest ship and searched until it brought in Kurstand Baldassar, standing on the bridge. Beside him was the ablest naval officer in the Marmaduke's command, Lord High Admiral Coltrain, a veteran whose grizzled hair and erect ruggedness attested to his long and rigorous life. Ted felt a pang of distaste at the stern necessity which would in a few moments cause him to destroy this brave sailor whose name had been a household word for a generation. Nor was the least of his reputation due to his open defiance of some of the Marmaduke's cruellest measures at a time when that tyrant could ill afford to lose his services.

"Baldassar," called Ted through his enunciator, "and you Coltrain, do you hear me?"

The Grand Marshall looked stonily before him, but Admiral Coltrain slightly inclined his head.

"You have seen the effect of my projector upon your aeroplanes. You can well imagine the result if I turn it upon but one of your ships. I dislike to take a million lives, as you must know I should. If there is any honor left in the Marmaduke's fleet, I will give it a chance to turn back. Toss overboard every pellicule you carry and set forth to the east at full speed ahead. Keep your ships together. If you disobey, you will immediately be destroyed.

"Baldassar, do you assent." The immobile features of the generalissimo might have been cast in bronze.

"Coltrain, as chief naval officer, can you speak for the fleet?" The Admiral's face was leaden gray as he peered toward the challenger. Slowly he nodded his head in an affirmative.

"Remember, Admiral, my directions must be fully obeyed. No turning back, no separating of the fleet." Again, the Admiral nodded grimly. The ships began to wheel about, as neat a manoeuvre as Ted had ever hoped to witness. Yet he was harassed by grave doubts as to whether he should allow this threat to his country's safety to exist at all. Coltrain, he felt, could be trusted, but Baldassar might supersede his authority.

He was mortally tired now, and fantastic pictures flashed across his mind. What would prevent the enemy fleet from splitting up and returning to devastate the seacoast cities from North and South? He could see Coltrain dead or in chains, and Baldassar smiling at the work of destruction.

Suddenly, a huge red flare glowed to the eastern horizon, dimming the greyer light of morning. Repercussions of air rocked his plane as though it were cradled on desperately high waves, until the stout braces of the wings groaned under the strain and threatened to snap. A mighty suction of air was carrying him rapidly seaward while beneath him waves, mountainously high, were rushing inshore, their tops churned with angry froth. He must make a higher altitude quickly or he would be caught in the roaring mass. Then, when he had done all he could, they passed close under him, lashing him with foam, with valleys between the crests that seemed to lay bare the ocean floor.

When Ted reached an altitude which put him out of immediate danger, he set his televisor to bring in the location of the Marmaduke's fleet. To his astonishment, at a range much closer than the fleet should have been if they had obeyed his instructions, great masses of shining metal were dropping into the ocean.

So that was the end of the Great Invasion. An immense sense of relief swept through the lone aviator, tempererd with a deep horror at the destruction of more than a million men even though they had advanced against his country with deadly purpose. He was nauseated by a powerful stench like that of overripe bananas. Later, he remembered nothing of his flight back to Washington, except that he had a severe ache in his chest.

The pain had become a dull numbness when Ted next opened his eyes. A young woman in a spotless uniform hovered over him. She was pretty, but he preferred to shut his eyes and let the languorous softness of his surroundings soothe his tired nerves into an illusory sense of utter comfort. An uncompleted image, aroused by the nurse, struggled through his feeling of security.

"Where is Beatrice?" he demanded.

At the sound of his voice, the nurse startled. "You must be quiet for a while, Mr. Hardy," she said in a low tone. "Can you breathe normally?"

Ted was flattered by her respectful manner. He took a deep breath that seemed to open up recesses in his lungs which had long been closed.

"I'm a bit dizzy, but alright."

"Aren't you hungry?" asked the nurse with a smile.

"Yes. But let me ask one question. Where is Beatrice?"

"Miss Fairkind? I don't know," The nurse's face was serious and understanding. "She left for Washington last week, but her arrival hasn't been reported."

"Last week! Was she alone?"

"Of course. She has a transport license." The nurse held up her hand. "No, you can't get up."

"But there are spies about. Didn't one try to shoot us? I've got to tell somebody. Let me!"

The nurse held him firmly with one capable arm. Over her shoulder, Ted saw Beatrice, unsmiling, in the doorway.

"How are you, Mr. Hardy?" she asked. "Sorry if I am interrupting you."

"I'm feeling fine," said Ted, still dizzy.

"It was nice work, Ted. Just about the finest I ever heard of. When they told me that you were asking for me, I thought the least that I could do would be to come. Now I think I had better go."

"Please stay, won't you?" asked Ted hungrily. She came and sat on the far edge of his bed. Ted held out a shaky arm to her. "Just a little closer," he begged. "I have wanted to ask you something very personal."

"Yes," breathed the girl almost inaudibly.

Ted slowly raised his hand to the white curve of her shoulder and fumbled with a tiny silk ribbon which he located just under the egg-shell satin of her waist. He finally lifted the glass vial from its secret hiding place and held it to his cheek, still warm from her bosom. After a moment, he dashed it against the wall where it broke into many pieces.

"Promise you will never keep one of those again."

A heavy flush spread over her face. "With so much to wish for, is that what you really want?"

The look of exasperation in Beatrice's face sent a glow of warmth through Ted. He hugely enjoyed the fact that these Class A girls were so very human. At least Beatrice was. He liked temper in a girl, just about so much.

"What else," he asked her, "could I expect form the one girl who could put her country in danger and then who saved it by her own efforts?"

"Oh, but you and the professor are the only ones who know it was my invention which you used. Isn't that just a woman's lot?" she continued regretfully. "The only notice given me by the newspapers during the crisis was that I am lost. And even that was wrong. Actually, I was looking for a plane."

"But it was your discovery which turned Marmaduke's fleet," declared Ted indignantly. "Why didn't you let them know?"

"You see, there is a story to that. The professor was all for announcing the details of *his* invention to his fellow scientists. He did help me, of course, to assemble the apparatus. But the thing was too deadly, and publication of the formula would allow even the Marmaduke to equip with it. Professional enthusiasm is what he called it, -- blah, professional swelled-headedness. So I told the professor that he might have full credit for the discovery as long as he kept quiet about the formula, and no longer."

"Good girl!" Ted's eyes were starry in admiration. "I begin to see what Class A really means."

"So now they are erecting a monument to the professor at one end of the hall, facing across to yours. Courage and Science, America's protection. Isn't that nice?"

"A monument! Then I won't be court-martialled for proceeding without orders?"

"I guess not. Congress, by a special enactment, has raised your status from Class IV to Class I. It's the best thing they have done this session."

"You don't mean it, Then I can marry a Class A girl?"

"Certainly. You are really expected to." Beatrice rose to go.

"Wait a moment. Come over here," he demanded.

Beatrice seated herself again, remotely.

"Could I, for instance, marry you?"

Beatrice looked at him for a tense moment. "Perhaps."

"Can I?"

"Yes," she said so softly that Ted wondered if she had spoken at all.

"Well," he experimented, as he leaned forward, "we ought to have a son who will turn the scorpion's tail in the next big scrimmage, if any."

"Don't," said Beatrice, nestling her head in the hollow of his shoulder, "don't let's talk of future wars."

BURNT BRIDGES

Molly Anderson opened the door and peered through the misty darkness toward the shadow which was the road. Hidden in the glade, the crickets, clocking with merciless fingers the waning hours of summertime, paused for a moment to listen with her.

She turned, finally, to throw herself down on the table, her firm young arms outstretched over the strawberry spread. The red cloth seemed to catch a lurid glow from the oil lamp, or possibly, from her own frightened thoughts. She shuddered slightly, and waited.

At length her anxiety was rewarded. Down the road, not far away, came the sharp crackle of a gunshot, the muffled sounds of a violent scuffle and curses rising high into a wail.

"Oh God, " she cried, "he'll kill him!"

After a long moment, heavy footfalls approached the door and a heavy hand flung it open.

"Molly!" The girl looked up. "The coward tried to kill me. See? Here is his gun. I took it out of his hands as if he were a baby."

"Did you hurt him, father?" She forced her eyes to look into his haggard face.

"Did *I* hurt *him*?" he repeated incredulously. "No, I left him lying in the road. One can't thrash a drunken man. He's got that in store for him when he comes for the gun."

"We can't leave him in the road," said Molly, her voice trembling.

"You needn't worry," The old man's face hardened into a sneer. "His kind keep out of accidents."

"If only mother were here," wept Molly miserably.

The hard look stayed in the old man's eyes. "She might better be home taking care of her own, than out minding everyone else's sick. But mark this, she isn't here now, and *I'm* telling you that you won't see that fellow tonight."

"But I shall get him out of the road," said Molly with sullen determination. Her father seemed remote, ineffectual against the tide which welled up within her. She couldn't know how his blood leaped through his throbbing brain, afire with hard liquor and with the stubborn resentment which can be aroused in backwoods men when they feel their most inherent rights have been invaded.

"Molly," he cried, and his voice vibrated with an impotent suffering that cut deeper than rage, "would you go to that common loafer, who tried to kill me?"

But Molly had been swallowed by the night. A low groan followed her faintly from the house, and again the dirge of the crickets went on scornfully without interruption.

She found Mel astride a broken log, just off the road. He was, incredibly, whistling Rock-a-bye-baby.

"Hello, baby," he called as he pulled her down beside him. She was grateful for his strength, his sheer animal vigor.

"Mel," she confided, "I had to come. I feel as if I must be with you always. Don't you feel a little of that toward me?"

"Oh sure," said Mel, "why sure." And in her heart, Molly believed he meant it, or would at least until some stronger impulse came to cleave him from her. She must fortify against that cleavage, beginning with her father's wrath, which after all, had been the means of bringing them sooner together. Mel's hot head sought the cool of her bare arm. She petted his forehead possessively. This night had been created for them alone, and they for it. The rest of the world could for a moment be well forgotten.

A bright light to the west aroused them. They became aware of the heavily settling mists.

"You'll catch your death here," cried Molly in alarm. "Come, we must go back."

The light had become brighter, more lurid.

"That doesn't look like the head-lights of a car," remarked Mel as he stood up. "Seems to me more like fire."

"Hope it isn't my house!" exclaimed Molly, frightened. "There's only one other close enough to be that."

They hastened to a short rise in the road, only to confirm their darkest fears. Molly's house was in flames.

"Your old man did that," Mel accused. "He was mad enough to do anything."

They watched the fluid tongues of fire lap at the walls, the eaves, the open doorway. In a front window, the big geranium that her mother had loved stood for its last proud moment, ghostlike in the glare, until a hotter blast smothered it forever. It was all unreal and impersonal to Molly, as if she stood apart and saw it happen to another girl who had been herself. The heart inside of her almost exulted, because now there would be no necessity for postponing her choice. She was ready to go with Mel.

There was a new, a forced note of briskness in Mel's voice as he spoke, calling her out of her daze and away from the insufferable heat. "You'd better stay at my house tonight. In a day or two we'll drive into the city. You can find lots of things to do there."

"But I want to stay with you, always," she exclaimed in surprise.

"Some day, if I ever can afford to marry, we'll get tied up. You'll see if we don't, Molly."

"Some day! Oh, I see." Suddenly she realized that she had been giving constantly of herself. What had she gotten in return from any of them? Nothing -- nothing much. It had taken the fire to bring that out clearly. Her father, in his crude way, had been more successful than he had dreamed.

Her feet followed Mel because there was nowhere else to go. In the morning, she would begin a new, a wider life. There seemed to be nothing here except the damp clutch of the mists and the bleating crickets endlessly clocking the few remaining hours of summer.

IRIS

The tinkle of brass against steel, as a small object struck the radiator casing, unpleasantly smote the ears of Mr. Jonathan Rice. The missile, which proved to be the ornate cap belonging to young Mr. St. Claude's ink well, clattered along the lacquered top until it fell to the floor with an angry purr.

Mr. Rice let the grim lines which graved his face grow slightly deeper. Ever since January, when the elder St. Claude had bequeathed his tidy brokerage business to young Jerry, Jonathan Rice, who continued to hold his limited partnership, had eyed the growing restlessness of his new chief with disapproval. Nor were the minor partner's fears unjustified. In a business which makes a few, a very few important decisions during the year, and depends largely for its success upon the correctness of its judgements, even a small degree of impatience might prove ruinous.

Jerry, at the outset, had applied himself impetuously to his work, had tried to follow in the footsteps of his father, who was always considered a "safe" man. But since mid-April, a month ago, his actions began to undergo the change which was causing the lesser partner no little uneasiness. Jerry's attention had grown unaccountably formal and abstracted, and he deserted his desk for long periods. The gymnasium at his club accounted for much of his absence for he had always been a good, if not a brilliant athlete.

Not the least disturbing sign of the strange phobia which had lately possessed the young man was in his suddenly changing the position of his desk so that it faced away from the window where for years his father had watched the magnificent view of the harbor and its endless maritime parade. Mr. Rice, who hated change, couldn't understand this, especially when Jerry would come back to the window for long silent intervals to gaze at the ships and the sea. What Mr. Rice or, for that matter, anyone else may have thought on this sunny morning in May was of very little import to Jerry. If he chose to take a dislike to outgoing vessels and then to torment himself by watching them go, that was, chiefly, his own concern.

A vessel was moving out now, a large ship of the French line, majestically unconcerned with the and prejudices of the pygmies who watched from afar. Serenely, it belched forth a column of jet smoke that covered it like a huge feather. And Jerry, seeing this, was reminded of his Aunt Salome in her shadowy French chateau with its feather, and her Park Avenue apartment which promptly made unbearable the thought of staying in an oppressive office for another minute, so that he reached for his hat and left without a scant word to Mr. Rice. When he had gotten to the street level, where the canyon of masonry yawned deepest, he hailed the first taxi driver who passed.

"Uptown," he told the man. "Toward Central Park."

Whither he went wasn't important, he reflected, as long as he escaped the stifling mass of tall buildings. He leaned back luxuriantly and enjoyed the odor of spring.

At an intersection of Sixth Avenue, the cab stopped for a traffic light. If the signal had been green instead of red, this story could never have been written. On such flimsy trifles hang the fates of men.

So Jerry got out at Sixth Avenue, in the lower thirties, paid the cabby, and started cross-town on foot. It was when he stopped to light a cigarette that he saw her, and he looked closely because, almost against his will, the girl who walked ahead of him reminded him of somebody else. He noticed that she was young, too young, really, but the curve of her neck was completely satisfying, a circumstance which gave a pleasant focus to his thoughts. Almost at once she slipped out of sight into an open doorway, and Jerry prepared to cross the street.

Again, the light was red, so, taking advantage of the brief intermission, he noted the character of the place she had entered. It was a dingy old hole not worthy of a second glance, unless the drab sign "Employment Bureau" held anything in the way of promise. Jerry, while he finished his cigarette, took time to hope that anyone with so perfect a neck would not be forced to take some menial class of employment such as sewing buttons on pants or cracking nuts.

With a shrug of his supple shoulders, Jerry realized that he had troubles of his own and prepared once more to cross the street. At that instant, the girl reappeared with a speed that betrayed more spirit than dignity. Unfortunately her long heel turned on what appeared to be nothing, and dropped her to the sidewalk in a huddle which she contrived to make rather graceful, if slightly pathetic.

"May I?" exclaimed Jerry, offering to raise her.

She eluded him on the way up and turned a flushed face to his in which she seemed to accuse him as the cause of her mishap. There was a fiery quality in her eyes, vaguely disturbing to his curiosity.

"I am afraid," she said coolly, "I don't know you."

"Of course," he answered, "but I was afraid my unfortunately timed passing had been to blame and I wished to make amends."

"No," she answered, softening a little, "it wasn't your fault."

She looked past him, down the street, and of course the incident should have ended there. But as we know, Jerry wasn't going anywhere.

"If there is any way I could assist you," he said, mildly regretful, "perhaps call a cab?"

The girl looked at him, apparently for the first time. A frown clouded her face, she started to speak, but didn't.

"Say it," urged Jerry.

"I shouldn't," she flattered him with a moment of her interested attention, "but I am searching for some remunerative employment." Abruptly she colored as though this admission gave him an unfair advantage. "If you should know of something, I'd do anything decent."

Jerry pondered.

"Wait a moment," he exclaimed, "until I get a cab so we can go out to the Park where the air is fit to breathe. We can talk better there."

"No," said the girl quickly, "but if you wish, we will walk over to Fifth Avenue and take one of those open buses. They pass the Park, I believe."

"As you wish, Miss ---," Jerry bowed.

"Iris. Just Iris for the present."

"A pretty name. A flower, isn't it?"

"Yes. And the rainbow." Her voice tapered into a touch of bitterness. Jerry didn't like that.

"Oh, yes. Mine is Jerome, though I'd like it if you would call me Jerry. The other name," he hesitated for a briefly embarrassing interval, "is St. Claude."

"St. Claude," Iris repeated musingly. Then, bluntly, as she remembered, "didn't I see you in the tabloids last month? For running off to Europe with a married woman, wasn't it?"

Jerry winced under the color which deepened in his cheeks. "Not quite," he said weakly. "It was my picture alright but it wasn't a married woman, she was just going to be. And it wasn't Europe, it was North Africa. And she didn't marry me after all. And I didn't take her, it was another fellow. She was really leaving me for him."

"Oh! Is that on the level?"

"Of course, Iris."

"Then I'm sorry I brought it up, Jerry. Forgive me."

The way she said Jerry gave him such a warm twist inside that he almost did forgive her the rest of it.

"And now that we know each other a littler better, can't we take a taxi instead of the bus?"

"Why?"

"Because, frankly, I'm afraid of having my picture taken."

Iris considered this.

"No," she said finally. "Nobody would take it on so short a ride. Not if you weren't willing. It wouldn't be decent."

"You don't know those vultures," ventured Jerry grimly.

"Well, I'll take a chance if you will."

"Alright," But as they climbed atop a riverside bus, Jerry eyed the other passengers furtively. They seemed harmless enough. A mother and her small son, a couple of Italian laborers were all, but Jerry did get quite a turn when one of the men shifted his black lunch box which looked suspiciously like a camera.

They got off the bus at the Metropolitan Museum of Art. Without going inside, they slipped around the building, leisurely passed Cleopatra's Needle, and eventually reached the comparatively broad green expanse of the Meadow.

"Oh," exclaimed Iris, suddenly, "I must find one."

Disregarding the sign that forbade trespassing, Iris skipped over the greensward and crouched low with extended arms as if to gather it to her heart.

"See," she cried to Jerry as he came up. "I have found one the very first thing."

"What?" he asked her.

"Don't you know?" she asked in some disappointment. "A four-leafed clover, silly."

They bent over to examine it more closely. Jerry noticed that she had long tapering fingers and, though it was only May, her arms were nicely tanned.

"Don't you believe in signs?" The intruding voice was unpleasantly cynical. It emanated, they discovered, from a park patrolman who was holding himself a bit too tightly onto his chestnut colored mount.

Jerry eyed him critically. "Don't you know, sir," he said calmly, "that your circingle is loose?"

The policeman bridled. "Never mind the circingle. Just get off the grass." He moved his horse threateningly toward Jerry.

"Whose grass is this?" asked Jerry, rising in indignation. He hadn't stepped back as the horse came closer. In fact, his out-thrust chest had come in physical contact with that of the horse and it was the sensitive animal which swerved away from the man. The patrolman, as though catching the mood of his mount, also became undecided. After the unexpected failure of his frontal attack, he was plainly of two minds.

"We were just finding a lucky shamrock," Iris broke in. "Won't you accept it for a boutonniere?"

Again the young patrolman flushed, this time with pleasure. He took the clover gingerly from Iris and remarked with scarcely convincing authority, "You must mind the signs, but maybe you will find another on your way out."

He left them then, to slip behind a clump of shrubbery where he furtively tightened his saddle. As he did so, he muttered, "That chap certainly knows horses. I wonder who he is?"

Iris found two more lucky clovers before they reached a vacant bench at the edge of the sidewalk.

"Now," said Jerry, "tell me whatever you wish about yourself, and we will see what can be done."

"What I shall tell you will be very brief. Two months ago, I left my home for several reasons which were sufficient, at least to me, but which I shan't trouble to mention now. I had enough money to last a couple of months, and I have a little of that, but not much left.

"My hope was to become an artist who could actually paint pictures. Some of my teachers at home had been kind enough to flatter me a little and since I came here I have been fortunate to discover the greatest instructor in New York -- Herr Albert von Francken. He seems to like my work and is giving me instructions for a very moderate fee.

"Now I have come to the point where I must earn some more money, or," her foot tattooed the sidewalk impatiently, "or just or."

Jerry was filled with an impression of a pair of violet blue eyes that had suddenly grown darker.

"I think I can help you," he told her meditatively. "I'm a business broker. What is the proposition?"

"I should like to borrow five hundred dollars. That would be fifty dollars a week for ten weeks. It would, of course, be strictly on a business basis."

"Of course," agreed Jerry gravely, "could you give me any collateral?"

"I would sign a paper."

"Both names?"

"Certainly."

"Then I will grant the loan on one condition. Will you let me keep in touch with your progress in your work?"

Iris was silent for a moment. "I suppose that would be only fair, " she answered finally.

Jerry occupied himself for the next few minutes with his check book and fountain pen. He also drew up a promissory note for Iris to sign.

"Iris Stevens," read Jerry, "now that our business has been concluded, may I invite you to lunch?"

"You may lunch with me but I shall make the condition this time. You are to be my guest. I am really grateful to you."

Iris still insisted on the open bus. They stopped at a crossing in the lower thirties and walked westward for a block or two until they came to a gray stone hotel building trimmed with iron grillwork. It had orange and green awnings and the entrance was flanked by clipped bay trees.

A red-haired young man at the desk looked up as they entered and seemed to smile at Iris, although when he saw her companion his expression changed and he busied himself importantly with his work. Iris slipped over to exchange a few words with him which modified the frown but did not erase it. Iris' smile, as she returned to Jerry's side, was puzzling.

"I hope you won't mind, Iris, if I tell you something." Jerry's tone became low and confidential after they had been seated in the dining hall. "It's better not to get too well acquainted with chaps like the one outside. They are likely to be predatory with girls from -- from outside New York."

"Go ahead and say it," said Iris hotly. "I know what you chosen people think of the rest of us. I have lived only in Buffalo, a wilderness half the size of Brooklyn, and in Chicago which is scarcely larger than Manhattan and the Bronx. But I have been in Palm Beach where I found that even New Yorkers are not too proud to be seen."

"I'm sorry," exclaimed Jerry facetiously. "All those cities are very admirable, perhaps more admirable in many ways than New York which, I may say, is not my home as I live in New Jersey. But please do not forget my warning that many of the young men you may meet here are inclined to be predatory."

"Are you predatory?" Mr. St. Claude?" asked Iris abruptly.

Jerry looked into her eyes for a moment and saw that they were sparkling dangerously. "No, but I could be," he answered with candor.

* * *

"How do you really like von Francken, Iris?" Elsa McReynolds, her black hair propped against a mulberry cushion, suddenly threw down the detective story she had been reading and regarded Iris with fixed attention.

Iris, interrupted in a reverie, turned to her roommate with some surprise for it had been Elsa who, wise in the inner secrets of the city's art circle, had first recommended von Francken as the best teacher of oil painting which the city afforded.

"Frankie is a dear, even though he does growl like an angry bear. But I have found him out, Else. He is afraid -- afraid, because he is so human, that his feelings will spill over and people will discover them and laugh."

"But do you think he is really helping you, Iris? You know what I mean. Art is all right, but one must make a living."

"He complimented me today, Elsa, and he almost never does that. He said I had a fine sense of proportion. That comes from daddy -- you have heard of Huntington Stevens, the engineer. And he said I had a natural fondness for beauty. That was what my romantic mother did for me. But, Elsa, it's more than a fondness, it's an intenseness, a yearning, a fluttering of wings against iron bars in the darkness, struggling for a chance to show their colors in the light.

"Yet Frankie always spoils his compliments. He said I am too volatile, too easily diverted, to become a fine artist. He told me I must experience more of life!"

"He always did that," Elsa shrugged. "He likes to egg them on."

"He doesn't know! I'll show him, Elsa. I have an idea, but I couldn't tell even you about it now or it might slip away. Could you pose for me a little?"

"I am under contract with Artemis Fashions, Inc. not to pose for anyone else, Iris. You know it."

"This isn't commercial, Elsa. It would be just for me. And it won't be you in the picture, I promise you that."

"Maybe. But now, Iris, let me ask you something. About this Jerry fellow who stops for you every Wednesday. Is he paying your way?"

"I have had a loan from him," said Iris, coloring, "if that is what you wish to know."

"What? Oh, Iris, you should have asked me. You don't know this big bad city. After you have been here two years, as I have, you will be a lot more careful."

"It is altogether a business proposition," she said stiffly.

"But Iris, Mr. Perry, the manager, has had his eye on him and he is worried about you, and Mr. Maxwell, when I told him about it, said that it was a shame and someone ought to tip you off."

"Why, Elsa! I suppose you were sitting in the sheerest of understandings while the talented Mr. Maxwell paused from his sketching to wipe a couple of tears from his eyes for the poor little girl who had no one to tell her," Iris couldn't refrain from an ironic smile. "And what an evil town this is for a girl who is all alone. And my hair-dresser said as much last Tuesday, not to mention Mr. Murphy, the houseman who told me to keep an eye on that fellow."

"Well, Iris," said Elsa, loyally, "If you say it is all right that goes with me, kid. But do be careful."

"Don't worry. You can learn things in places outside New York. I did. Just now I'm thinking of nothing so much as the picture that I want to paint. You will pose, won't you?"

Elsa leaned over and patted Iris on the arm. "Sure, kid." When Elsa had safely immersed herself again in her mystery story, Iris resumed her reverie where it had been interrupted. Herr von Francken had spoken golden words that day and she revelled in the memory of them.

"Color, harmony, proportion and soul," she remembered, "and the greatest of these is soul. It is the final gift of the gods. Without it is only a shell. Don't ever lose it. Don't ever let them take it away from you. They are so eager, the wolves, to buy it for a mess of -- what do you call it -- cornflakes."

"But is that not art -- to paint a breakfast food?" Iris had asked.

"Ach, but yes. I have so done, when I must -- what do you call it -- keep the kettle boiling. Honest goods, honestly portrayed, it is all right. But it is also easier to be clever than to be great. So few of us can do the important things, and fewer yet can afford to do them. But perhaps it is you."

"No, Herr Franken, I am not rich. To be very frank, I am in debt."

"Ah, but that may be your good fortune. One does nothing unless there is someone or something over him to crack the whip. We are so pitifully human."

Today, he had comforted her so much. As usual, she had come away with a little glow of enthusiasm somewhere deep inside of her. Again she could see sunny green valleys filled with many people who were content because each loved his own labor and perhaps, too, because he trod in the shadow of a beautiful old cathedral with its high pointing spires and its still challenging nobility of architecture. Some day, she secretly hoped, her own little glow might burst forth in an achievement worthy of so great a teacher.

PENUMBRA

* * *

At ten o'clock on Friday morning, Else reclined n the raised dais in Iris' smallish studio room. Her skin was ivory against the dark curtain which formed the background and Iris, allowing her artistic appreciation full swing, was painting rapturously.

"Funny thing, Iris, you probably wouldn't believe it, but this is the first time I have ever stripped. Always had a feeling that it would be unlucky. Still," said Elsa pensively, "If you ever get good, I should like to hang in the Metropolitan. So far, I've stared at myself in gowns and scanties on theatre programs, bill posters, car ads and in millions of magazines but now I'm thinking how wonderful it would be to have a few of those bearded papas, who know everything, shake their heads a little over my picture and say, 'That's good, very nice color and form.' After all, that's the real thing," she ended pensively.

Iris painted in silence for some minutes, her brow puckered in her deep attention. Else, who had not yet been permitted to see the unfinished painting was consumed by a growing curiosity.

"Couldn't I take one little peek?" she asked. "It wouldn't be bad medicine if only I should look."

"Nobody," said Iris firmly, "will see this picture until it is finished. But you will be the first. That's a promise."

Elsa pouted, and pulled the dark hangings about her until she was completely covered, and so she did not hear the knock at the door which Irish had instantly recognized as of Jerome St. Claude. Presently, when she did become aware of the commotion and peered out from the soft velvety folds, she was gravely concerned to observe a young man entering at the door which had carelessly been left unlocked, while Iris was too much occupied in hiding her uncompleted work to notice the plight of her unfortunate model.

"I'm sorry to disturb you," Jerry apologized, surprised at the annoyance which he read in the girl's flushed countenance. "I have had the Falconette out on the sound, and she is running beautifully . Perhaps you would like to take a weekend cruise with me."

"Am I to consider this a proper request?" asked Iris.

Again Jerry was uncertain of the tone of her voice. Even the color of her eyes had changed, becoming like two dark pools of violet. Nor did the sun-browned features reveal any secrets of the real person behind them.

"I can't make up my mind about you," she told him candidly. "I'm not even sure I like you, and we might bore each other dreadfully during so many hours."

"We couldn't," said Jerry confidently. "Would you mind my Aunt Salome?"

"I think I should insist on your aunt, but why Salome?"

Jerry laughed. "She is my favorite aunt, but she isn't so much like Herod's favorite dancer. Guess they picked Salome by mistake when they should have selected Esther. She is one of the few really dignified people left since the war and prohibition. You will probably like her."

"And you propose to take me miles from shore to find out?"

Jerry's face betrayed a pleasant dash of excitement when, without apparent reason, it clouded suddenly. Iris, following his glance with her eyes, had a quickening sense of remorse for the forgotten Elsa.

"Don't," she cried in growing panic, as he moved toward the enveloping curtain which bulged unexpectedly and seemed to quiver. "Please done take offense, but you must go out for a little while."

His eyes darkened with a flash of suspicion, but he turned away. "Very well," he said somberly, "I'll go."

He didn't go at once, because, barring his exit in the open doorway, was a blonde young woman. She was smartly, rather strikingly dressed in a gown of some dark and spidery design as of a delicately webbed creature in a warm swamp. Her attitude, her almost insolent smile commanded attention.

"Jerry," she was saying, "you've led me quite a chase, but this is worth it. Aren't you glad to see me? I've come back."

"Already, Hila?"

"Absolutely, Jerrykins. I couldn't go through with it, finally. Wilbur is a tiresome animal."

"You were fortunate to find out in time," ventured Jerry.

"Wasn't I. And when I saw the Falconette riding at anchor this morning I remembered how you promised me a long ride some day and I realized something else, that I guess I should have thought of before. I could never marry a man with whom I wouldn't be willing to spend a solid twenty-four hours, alone."

An involuntary motion of Jerry's head caused Hila to glance more definitely in the direction of Iris. Almost immediately she turned away, but not before a rapid glance of hatred had glinted from the steely blue eyes against the luminous pool of violet. The golden hair, audaciously, metallically, beautifully golden, shook roguishly in the manner of a child who has made an important discovery.

"Jerrykins, you naughty boy, I didn't realize about you. Why couldn't I have known before? It would have spared us -- well -- call it a bad dream!"

Her cheeks broke into dimples, she was, in a moment, all curves and ringlets. On her ears hung sparkling crescents that might well have been wrought from pirate's plunder. So far as Hila would indicate, Iris was merely another incident of the room, less even than the dainty chair upon which she had placed a ruthless foot, shod in the skin of an exotic lizard.

Iris wavered between a feeling akin to paralysis and a desire to send the insolent valkyrie outside where she more properly belonged. In the end, her curiosity won.

"On the whole, Jerry," Hila was saying, "I am glad this happened. Otherwise you might never have forgiven me. And I am here to tell you that even though I have been a truant, it was you, after all, who counted."

"Did it ever occur to you, Hila, that there are other people to consider beside yourself? For example, your husband."

It was Hila's turn to flush. "I suppose I do deserve some ironics. I expected that. There is no husband, thank goodness."

"I hold nothing for you but the kindliest regards, Hila. In fact, I am, if you understand me, grateful." His voice was level, fatal.

A brief shadow of consternation clouded her face, followed by a tightening of the little lines at the edge of her mouth. The smile became rigid but never faltered.

"You have grown, Jerome. We could be happier together now, I think, knowing what we have learned apart."

Hila managed a cigarette with a firmness which wrung from Iris a grudging admiration. Finally she spoke again in a voice which was almost humble. "Of course, I expected a drubbing but I thought you were still chivalrous to listen to my explanation. My car is waiting, Jerry. Won't you come?"

"You will excuse me if I do not see you down, Hila. My time is growing very short."

Iris was puzzled by the flash of sinister triumph which shot from the eyes of the other woman. Her "very well" was surprisingly devoid of the fury which Iris had rather expected would follow. "But you will come a little later," she added.

It as at the instant of Hila's departure that the luckless Elsa made a futile reach for her clothes.

"What's this?" exclaimed Hila as she pulled aside the light curtain, and then with deliberately chosen emphasis, "Sheik Jerry." Elsa fought vigorously to keep herself covered, and in the end, the screen fell upon her in a not too well concealed huddle on the floor.

"Don't you think, Jerome," said Hila triumphantly, "that we had better run along."

Jerry St. Claude made an exclamation under his breath which sounded like "blundering fool" as he grasped Hila and pushed her before him into the corridor. Over his shoulder, he called huskily, "I'll see you again, Iris, Later."

"I told you," said Elsa ruefully, when the door was finally locked, "it would be bad luck. My hunches are usually right."

"What a nice mess I have gotten into," Iris murmured with a reproachful glance towards the unfinished picture. "Whatever made me think I could paint."

* * *

At eleven o'clock, hard on the heels of Elsa's departure, Iris entertained her third visitor. He was a round man who wore dark tinted glasses, and, as soon as the door was opened, lost no time in entering.

"My name," he announced, "is Wakefield. Daniel Wakefield, the art dealer. You have heard of me?"

"No," said Iris.

"Well, no matter. I have some reputation here." He glanced about the room appraisingly. "May I see some of your work?"

"There is nothing to exhibit."

"Tch, tch. You are too modest." His eyes were getting about the room with surprising agility. Presently he discovered the canvas which Irish had faced against the wall. "What is this?" he asked, turning it.

"Don't do that," exclaimed Iris.

"Ah." He stood and inspected the painting, critically. "Very good work for an amateur. Very good, indeed. I think I have a market for that one. What would be your lowest price, young lady?"

"But the picture is unfinished," protested Iris, "and is not for sale."

"My client sometimes prefers them that way. More to the imagination, you know. He is rather eccentric. But in this case, I can assure you, my dear young lady, he is making no mistake. Have you not a use for ready money?"

"Well -- " Iris found herself attempting to overcome a feeling of dislike for the fellow.

"Two hundred dollars," he snapped briskly, "in cash."

Iris was unimpressed and plainly showed it.

"Three hundred."

She shook her head.

"Four hundred."

Iris remained silent.

"He may give five hundred. It would be the outside figure."

Iris considered. She no longer regarded the picture with the high enthusiasm which had animated her before the blonde Hila's visage and the embarrassing events of the morning. Even her interest in art seemed to have turned sour.

"I could use five hundred dollars," she said curtly. If anyone were so great a fool as to pay more for a picture than it could possibly be worth, that wasn't her concern.

"Now, Miss -- " he paused.

"Stevens."

"Oh, yes, Miss Stevens. Miss Stevens, if you do not object I shall take a snapshot of your picture, merely to corroborate my description of it to my client. No doubt he will like it and I can bring the money later."

Mr Wakefield brought out a small camera from his side pocket, placed it upon a table, and propped the canvas in front of the lens. Irish dropped into a chair and waited, indifferently, until he should go. She was vastly bored, for he seemed to be deliberately prolonging his operations, changing his camera about and occasionally pulling tabs. "To get the right angle," he told her.

"Are you taking my picture?" Iris asked him once.

"Oh no," he said quickly, and moved the camera.

At length Iris got up from her chair and stood suggestively at the doorway.

"There," said Mr. Wakefield, "I think I have it. You will hear from us soon." The man's tone was hollow, almost mocking.

"Good day," Irish shivered slightly when she closed the door. His round face and owlish eyes filled her with a sense of personal invasion even after he had gone.

Iris was not fated to be alone that morning. This time it was Jerry who knocked. He waited to be let into the studio and instead of seating himself with his customary casualness, he remained stiffly at the door. His lips were restless. Iris had never before noticed how sensitive they were, and he was having some difficulty in his attempt to speak.

"Who was just here?" he demanded.

"An art dealer. Daniel Wakefield."

"You think so? That's stumpy Judson. And you call him an art dealer" Did he take any pictures?"

"He said he would buy my painting for five hundred dollars when he comes back."

"No, I mean did he take any photographs. He isn't an art dealer, just a camera man for a questionable paper."

"Why he snapped a picture of my painting to show his client." Suddenly Iris flushed. "Oh, he probably did take one of me while he was fussing. Does it matter?"

Jerry saw Iris' startled eyes, her quivering chin, and reproached himself because he had doubted her.

"You never saw him before, did you?" he asked gently.

"Of course not. Why?"

"Someone sent him here," said Jerry evenly.

Jerry read the name that started to form on Iris' lips and nodded gravely.

"It must be Hila. That would explain a lot of other things, too. So many intimate happenings that have been distorted and printed in one particular scandal sheet. They could never have learned otherwise. Hila has been a vampire, a traitor to her friends, feeding on the hospitality of people who took her without question."

"What will happen now?" asked Iris in a toneless voice.

Jerry's face clouded. "Tomorrow we shall be published with insinuations and photographs."

"It's all my fault," exclaimed Iris, remorsefully. "It was so very plain I should have known at once."

Jerry regarded her inquiringly.

"That fellow couldn't be an art dealer because he was color blind. He was wearing a blue shirt with an atrociously purple tie."

"Let me see that picture, Iris."

She nodded toward the stand where her canvas was still propped as the photographer had left it. Two figures were delineated in the foreground, a youth and a maiden against a setting with appeared to be allegorical, but which was not fully developed. The youth was helping the girl over an impasse. The figures were nude. Jerry looked at the picture for a long time. His face as he turned again to Iris, had attained a deep color.

"Will you let me announce our engagement today?"

"You mean," she said listlessly, "That it will save you -- save us, rather -- a lot of embarrassment. Yes, I can be a good sport and I feel as though I owe you quite a lot."

"Must you put it that way?"

"Shouldn't we be honest with ourselves?"

"Thanks. I'll accept the burnt offering with gratitude but, Iris, I have another suggestion. Let's go ahead with our weekend cruise. To become better acquainted."

"With your Aunt Salome?" asked Iris.

"She will come, of course. And you could bring some friends if you wish. It's your party -- sweetheart."

"Did that last word come so hard?"

"Suppose it were an experiment that I had never tried before. But will you come?"

"I think Else would love to go. Anyhow she would worry about me if she didn't. And there is Freddie James, the room clerk at my hotel. He has read about so many yachts, it's time he actually experienced one."

"Good. We will start in the morning -- shall we say at nine? I can look in for you then."

"That will be very kind of you."

"And now since I seem to be dismissed, I shall go and notify the papers. We are still in time to spoil one little dish." He pressed Iris' chin gently between his fingers and drew it upward towards his face. "May I?"

Iris turned away. "Wait. Perhaps tomorrow, but not today," she said huskily.

Jerry, in closing the door, wondered if the sound he had heard was really a pent-up throat-catching sob.

* * *

Salome St. Claude was one of these rare individuals, who, without any particular effort, becomes the natural center of gravity in any group with which they happen to be identified. Before they had weighed anchor, she had put the mistrusting Mr. James both at ease and in his place by allowing him to light her cigarette and then, with a little pat on the back, telling him he was a nice boy. She had endeared herself to Else by telling her that she had been adorable in her latest showings for Artemis Fashions, Inc. For the briefest interval, she had placed her arm around Iris, and it wasn't an uncomfortable arm, either. "I like your aunt a lot," Iris told Jerry later.

After she had stirred up a clatter of conversation, and before it had a chance to grow strained, she said, "I know you young people don't want me to stay too closely so run along and enjoy yourselves." After that she spread out on the secretary in the lounge room, some unfinished business pertaining to one of her numerous clubs, and promptly forgot about them.

The four went to the forward deck to play a modified form of tennis, a game which proved so diverting that it consumed the greater part of the forenoon. Deck tennis and the salt air combined to whet appetites for lunch which were hearty, to say the least. Long Island duckling and soft shell crabs fried in butter were only a part of the tasty menu. As a fitting climax Jerry brought out a couple of bottles with musty labels dated back twenty or more years.

It was in the early afternoon that Salome St. Claude gave Jerry deep reason to feel grateful. She took Else to her bosom, figuratively speaking, perhaps for no less selfish a reason than to pump her skilfully about Iris, leaving the latter disengaged for the little heart to heart talk that Jerry had been anticipating with a mixture of eagerness and dread. Since Iris had not bothered to mention her engagement, it was apparent to Jerry that Freddy James might prove difficult. Shortly after lunch, however he was greatly reassured.

"Where is Freddie?" Iris asked when she and Jerry had settled into deck chairs and snugly wrapped themselves in blankets.

"I left him in his bunk." Jerry's eyes twinkled mischievously. "He has scooped up half a dozen cushions for comfort and he is trying to kill off the rest of the champagne. At least, he knows how to enjoy himself."

Iris frowned. "How long," she demanded, "Must this silly affair go on?"

"Aren't you enjoying yourself?"

"I mean our engagement."

"Until you marry me."

"But I shan't hold you to it. It was the best way out of unpleasant notoriety, wasn't it. I really owed you that much although I have decided not to marry anyone -- ever."

"But you must know that I have been entirely serious. I wanted you all the while."

"Where are we going?" asked Iris after a long but not unpleasant interval.

"Newport -- for the night."

"My father is there."

"I know," said Jerry, "I wired him." Then, as he saw Iris' quick look of surprise, he added, "Everyone knows of Huntington Stevens, the famous structural engineer."

Tears were gathering in her eyes, tears which were an indication of the turmoil of emotions within. They caused Jerry to remember his first encounter with her on Sixth Avenue where he had thought her so young, so pathetically young, an impression he had almost forgotten since.

"Do you know my mother, too?" Iris said presently.

"I am afraid not."

"She is in Florida. They both married again years ago, after the divorce."

"Oh," said Jerry, understandingly.

"I wanted to lose myself in a career," said Iris forlornly. "I didn't want my life to be like that."

"Do you mind if I tell you something rather personal?" He turned his head as though he were a trifle ashamed.

"Why, no, Jerry."

"When I was a little fellow, I used to dream about a girl with yellow hair. Quite often. We'd have an airship. Silly, wasn't it? But Hila reminded me of her and I nearly walked the plank before I came to my senses. Nearly, but not quite. I thought I had passed her on quite safely, and I still feel justified in the attempt.

"But when I met you I realized that Hila was only reminding me of you whom I had never seen. Funny, isn't it? But it's true. You needn't give up your career if you marry me. Maybe we can help each other more than ever."

Iris turned her face to the white-flecked water. "If you do take me," she warned, "you must not forget that you are taking my temper as well."

"What good is the pie without the seasoning," observed Jerry happily.

"I wouldn't care for anyone," confided Iris, "who couldn't stand up against opposition, at least once in a while." Perhaps she was thinking of the episode of the patrolman's horse. "And we won't always be quarrelling," she promised, as the last barrier fell away.

STRIPPED

Like many another man, Hugh McDonald has wondered what it would be like if he ever found a gun levelled at his chest. Now, as he sat on the edge of his smartly made hotel bed and looked down the short but sufficient barrel into the unsmiling face behind it, his face betrayed a mixture of fright and anger. Anyone who valued life so little as to take it with the flick of a finger was, in his opinion, worse than a rat, nor was his conviction changed by the fact that he person behind this particular revolver was a woman.

She had startled him with her sudden appearance at his door when he had been expecting someone else. The fury which blazed in her young face caused him to back cautiously away until he had sprawled foolishly over his own bed.

"What do you want?" he exclaimed sharply.

"First of all," she demanded in a low determined voice, "strip!"

"Really," he objected, "I'm very unromantic when I'm stripped."

"This isn't romance," she reminded him, "this is more serious business." Here eyes were ruthless. The gun quivered in her hand.   The red signals of wrath were mounting on his cheeks as he tore away his shirt, his undergarment, revealing a smooth, and almost hairless chest. His relief was great when the girl, modestly, allowed him his trousers. She stepped closer and peered at the pale blue markings tattooed over his heart.

"I see it's there," she remarked cynically.

"Oh, you knew?"

"She told me about it, but I wanted to be sure. The two initials, the twining flowers. Life must have been sweet and rosy then."

"It could have been, was," he admitted, "for a short, a very short time. Your mother, I think, tired first. Then she married your father. Not an altogether satisfactory arrangement, I understand."

"What did *your* wife think of the decoration?"

He winced. "She never bothered to inquire. Tattooing for sentiment went out long ago."

He was searching her face curiously. She was too much her mother's daughter for him to be mistaken. There were the same spritely contours, the too blonde beauty, the same savage reaching for happiness which had first drawn her mother to him and which had proven so baffling when she had become nearly though not quite his own. More pronounced in the daughter, the minute lines of her expression betrayed two warring natures, a growing hardness and an unsatisfied yearning. Even her eyes were mismatched, not in color but in mood, for while one was blazing defiance, the other drooped as if already repentant.

"Did you know at the start?" he asked, still almost incredulous.

"Yes, I opened your letter. My name is Gertrude, too. She's told me what you'd be like." Her voice, cool and dispassionate, suggested that the bitter processes of disillusionment had already begun.

Here, if experience had taught him anything about women, was fruit ripe for the plucking. A new female sprang out of the embers of his memory. Every woman, he believed cynically, had her price and he had money now, the link in his chain of happiness which had been so tragically missing when he and the other Gertrude had been very young. That one owed him something for spoiling what was the best part of his life. Well, let the daughter pay.

"How much," he asked her calmly, "is on the gun?"

"Five hundred dollars."

"Why didn't you ask. I should have been glad to have given generously to your mother's daughter."

"I didn't want to ask. I'd rather take -- from you." She noticed his conciliating shrug and continued more mildly, "but I'm not so sore as I was. I guess you weren't all to blame. She's tried through, tried her damnedest to make me happy."

Her face softened a bit, and the resemblance to the Gertrude of his past brought a stab of pain to Hugh McDonald.

"Here is double. Five hundred for the gun and five hundred for a kiss. Come, tell me how you will spend it."

"Mostly for Mother. She's ill, now. I want enough to get me away somewhere to start all over again, clean."

"Don't go away. I want to help you." He held his arm toward her invitingly.

The girl tossed the gun on the bed beside them and unexpectedly threw her arm about his shoulders, a prelude to the soft brush of her lips against his cheek. His hatred evaporated into a warm glow inspired partly by the memories she was arousing, yet even more by contact with her lissom young body.

"I shouldn't do this," she was saying, "but we will probably never meet again."

His arm sought to gather her closer, but she eluded him. "Good bye -- dad." Her smile was mirthless, mocking.

Hugh McDonald clutched the bed with convulsive fingers, hardly realizing that she could have gone so quickly. This girl, after all, might be his daughter, a fact that could easily ruin him, hold him up to unbearable ridicule. From what he had seen, she might be capable of anything. His wife -- God, if she ever knew. His fingers closed hysterically upon the weapon which lay beside him, while a force, quite apart from his reason, pushed the cold muzzle against the blue spot over his heart. He pulled the trigger before he realized what he was doing, and then he fairly screamed. With trembling fingers, he examined the gun more closely. It was unloaded.

SECTION 2

The Poems of Conrad Richard Kolbe

THE RIDDLE

O sea, which whispers strangely to the sand,

Enfolded in the rocks thy tale is told
How man-in-promise crawled in ages old
When shaky legs set forth to scale the land.
From primal cell to wak'ning brain are spanned
The records, as man's progress doth unfold.
Prophetic of that day which fate must hold. --
Ocean and desert mute, the world unmanned.

Tell me whence came the quick-ning touch, O sea?
Who sent the eons on their pregnant paths?
Who shaped the puny strain of men who pass,
Careless of each, tenacious of the whole?
Locked in thy hov'ring breast, for aye -- the key,
Hid in thy green-gray depths and trembling roll.

ON THE DEATH OF A BABY

Dear babe, who came but made so brief a stay,

Where is the wisdom, that in thy loved form,
Could make such promise unto us who mourn,
Yet wrench thy guileless soul so soon away?
If thou art better dead, why then wert born
To struggle here with numbing anguish torn
And vanish from us like the morning's ray?

Captains or cattle -- which? or some of each --
Are we who sow with joy and reap in tears?
What recompense for these, our yearning years,
When Heav'n is shown us -- though beyond our reach?
Time can assuage its wounds and numb the pain;
Deep in the heart its barbs will still remain.

Where'er the trial of men its path has led,
From fertile plain to grassy bank and hill,
The giant shadows of his forebears still
Tramp by his side, and with him Earth retread.
With grizzled hands they point the way ahead,
The hour-glass turned, fresh sands its globe refill
"Err not as we, new hope in you instil,"
Thus speaks the birthright that in men is bred.

PENUMBRA

A mighty drama, passing on through time,
The fates have spun across the lives of men.
Risen from dust, 'tis still their task to climb
Where knowledge dimly lights their passing day.
Still giant shadows urge them on their way,
Bidding them look beyond their clouded ken.

MY DREAM SHIP

My thoughts are not at home today -- they roam,

Caught by an engine whistle's shrill appeal,
And singing rails under the iron wheel;
Or on a white hulled steamer trail the foam,
Where salt-green lather whips the coral loam
My dream ship rides the waves with prying keel;
Where tropic skies their brilliant hues reveal,
Through palms and blossoms of some island home.

Then let the world spin on its circling track,
While in blest freedom, I would flee the strife,
The petty bustle of a work-day life,
And soothe my soul in Nature's calm estate,
But, in the end, my thoughts come trooping back
                Content again to labor and to wait.

SECTION 3

Family Memories and History by Eunice Kolbe Ross (daughter of Conrad Richard Kolbe)

The Courage of Elizabeth Nauman Kolbe (Big Dad's Paternal Grandmother)

Big Dad's paternal grandfather, Justus Kolbe, owned a ship and sailed it as captain. He and his wife Elizabeth Nauman Kolbe had five children. Their oldest child, Richard Edward Kolbe, eventually married and fathered Conrad Richard Edward Kolbe. However, all other members of the family died a tragic death.

The father Justus was sailing his trading ship with cargo to Brazil's big coffee exporting port, Santos. During an epidemic in 1877 Justus contracted typhoid fever and was dead in three days.

It was then that his wife Elizabeth set out to Brazil to protect her family's interests. On the last leg of her journey home, she boarded the Pommerania, one of Germany's biggest and best steamer ships. A tramp ship coming out of Liverpool, a large English port, with everyone aboard drunk, rammed the Pommerania off Fokestone and accidentally sank it (November, 1878).

Elizabeth started to get on a life boat but she stepped aside and gave her place to a woman with a child. No more boats came and the ship went down. Forty-three lives were lost, including Elizabeth.

Her oldest son Richard (Big Dad's father) was eight years old and a sensitive child. No one had the heart to tell him that his mother had drowned. Every day he went down to the large Hamburg seaport and watched for the ship that would bring his mother back. Finally a sailor could stand it no longer and told him the truth. The news knocked the child out and he remained in bed for eight weeks.

The Pommerania

Figure 3-1. The Pommerania.

The Pommerania was built in 1873 for the Hamburg-Amerika Line, an iron steamship of 3382-tons, measuring 120m x 14m. She had 600hp two-cylinder engines with single screw giving a top speed of 13 knots. The accommodation comprised of 100 1st, 70 2nd and 600 3rd class passengers.

According to one account, the Pommerania was sailing from New York to Hamburg via Plymouth in November 1878; she stopped off at Plymouth to offload some of the passengers and $7500 gold and then continued her journey through the channel. Unfortunately as she was travelling off the coast of Folkestone, carrying 109 passengers and 111 crew, she was hit by the iron-hulled barque *Moel Eilian* just before midnight on the 25th November 1878. The Pommerania was badly damaged and immediately began taking on water. Four of the nine lifeboats were destroyed in the collision and the other five had to try to take all the crew and passengers. One of the lifeboats was so crowded that it too sank. The steamer Glengarry came to the Pommerania's aid and saved many of the passengers. The Pommerania then took so long to sink that some of the passengers returned to rescue their possessions, but unfortunately the ship suddenly sank taking those people with her.

The Pommerania today is a well-known dive site off Dover on the south-eastern coast of England. The wreck lies on the port side at 27m on a seabed of cobbles, gravel and shell fragments. The ship is well broken but parts of the wooden deck are still intact. Some gold and silver coins have been recovered from the passenger accommodation. There are many clock mechanisms in boxes in holds. Visibility is often a good 4 meters. The wreck supports a large amount of sea life including sponges, anemones, mussels, bib, wrasse, tompot blennies, edible and swimming crabs and starfish.

Figure 3-2. The Pommerania today under the sea.

The Life of Richard Edward Kolbe (Big Dad's father) and his Siblings

by Eunice Kolbe Ross

*F*ollowing the tragic death of his father in 1877 and then his mother in 1878, young Richard Kolbe was adopted by an uncle (Nauman) and brought up in Hamburg, Germany. He had a cousin his age with whom he got into lots of mischief. Bid Dad remembered his father telling stories about their naughty behavior. Here is one of them.

One day young Richard and his cousin were throwing stones at a church in a hollow in a bank. As they shot down at the windows and hit them, they said, "Ping!"

Richard's uncle came up from the rear unnoticed by the naughty boys until he knocked their heads together and said, "Ping!"

Once the Haganback Circus came to town and was quartered in Hamburg. A camel escaped and a crowd chased it. Young Richard and his cousin merrily joined the chase. Richard ran into a long horse hitch on a wagon and split his head open. Remarkably, he survived.

Here is a story that Conrad couldn't tell without laughing. It happened one time when his father Richard was still a boy in school. Young Richard had misbehaved and was scheduled for a paddling the following day with the school's wooden paddle. The day he was to receive his punishment, his brother Fred helped him load up with several pairs of pants, vests, and shirts to soften the blows. But when he went to school that day, a substitute teacher was there who decided to practice physical fitness and had the students climb a smooth pole. Richard couldn't climb it and took off a jacket, revealing yet another jacket underneath it.

The teacher said, "What is that? Take off another layer!" One by one, as the teacher instructed him to remove another layer, off came the various coats, shirts, and pants.

Eventually, when the teacher told him to remove yet another pair of pants, Richard turned beet red. "I can't!" he cried. "This is my last one."

Following the tragic death of his father by typhoid fever in Brazil in 1877 and his mother's death during the sinking of the Pommerania in 1878, the rest of Richard's siblings (Fred, Bertha, Charlotte, and Gustave) also died quite tragically in this manner: Sister Charlotte died of typhoid fever in Germany. Sister Bertha moved to Oswego, New York, and worked as a household aid to a wealthy family as a young girl. But one day she went out on a boat alone on Onondaga Lake and drowned. Fred, who had followed Bertha to America, joined the American Army at Fort Niagara. There he died of typhoid fever. Gustave, the youngest sibling and barely out of his teens was also in the American army and was the first man killed in the Spanish American War. His rifle also fired the first shot of that war. An estimated 10,000 people attended his funeral and for years his grave was a separate island of honor in Woodlawn Cemetery in Syracuse.

Richard came to America as a super cargo (in charge of a cargo for a ship) which came into New York City. He had a few days off and had come up to Oswego to visit his sister Bertha, of whom he was a favorite. When he saw beautiful Onondaga Lake, white with sails and crystal clear water, he thought it was the most beautiful of lakes and decided to stay in America and make his home nearby.

Richard married Lillian Surbeck, daughter of John Conrad Surbeck and Margaret Ochsner, both from Lower

Rhinefall on the Rhein River in Switzerland but relocated to Syracuse, New York. John Conrad Surbeck (Grandpa Surbeck) had come to America from Switzerland at age 20 in 1857. A few years later he joined the army under General Sheridan during the Civil War. For part of that time, he became the body guard for General Custer. After the war, he retired from the military and owned a prosperous feed mill in Syracuse. He also purchased land and owned a lot of Eastwood and gave land to the Methodists for their Eastwood Church. He named Rigi Ave in Eastwood for the beloved mountains of his youth.

John and Margaret had one daughter, Lillian Margaret Surbeck, who married Richard Kolbe. They resided at 404 Highland Street. Richard Kolbe owned the first automobile in Syracuse (French-made before the American cars). He had to be pushed up hills and therefore liked to drive to the relatively flat North Syracuse. When he broke down (which was often) farmers laughed at him and yelled, "Get a horse!"

Richard's mother-in-law Margaret Ochsner Surbeck, had a sister named Barbara Ochsner who didn't marry. My father (Big Dad) referred to his great aunt Barbara as a "saint" who loved to tell stories to children. I saw her only once and was forever impressed that she felt such a kindred spirit for children and was so delighted to be with us. She thought children were special and we knew that she was. No earthly adult has impressed me more or left a stronger impression on my life. I was four at the time she died.

Figure 3.3 Barbara Ochsner, Big Dad's beloved great aunt Barbara, who never married. She taught Sunday School at what is now Westminster Presbyterian Church.

Interestingly, when Minabelle's good friend Ada died in the late 1980's, Uncle Bud found that her bible was inscribed as a gift from the church and her Sunday School teacher, Barbara Ochsner.

Figure 3.4 Obituary of Richard Edward Kolbe (Big Dad's father)

From Syracuse Newspapers, May 1924

RICHARD E. KOLBE

Richard E. Kolbe, 54, of 404 Highland Street, pioneer automobile dealer and later an investment broker in this city who died yesterday at his home, will be buried in Woodlawn Cemetery. Private funeral services will take place at 2 o'clock tomorrow afternoon at the home.

Born in Germany, Mr. Kolbe was graduated from Heidelberg University before coming to this country. He obtained the first Ford agency in Central New York and was also the first Syracusan to own a foreign built car. Retiring from the automobile business, he conducted an investment and brokerage office until his retirement some time ago.

Surviving are his wife, a son, Conrad R. Kolbe, a daughter, Miss Helen E. Kolbe, and a grandson, Conrad R. Kolbe, Jr.

RICHARD KOBLE, FORMER AUTO BROKER, DIES

Resident of Syracuse for 33 Years Passes Away at Home at Age of 58

Richard Kolbe, fifty-eight, for thirty-three years a resident of Syracuse and for many years a dealer and financier in the automobile business, died today at his home, No. 404, Highland Street after a brief illness.

Mr. Kolbe was lately associated with Morris Tanner and dealt in local securities with offices in the First Trust and Deposit Building and is said to have owned one of the first automobiles in Syracuse.

He was the son of Mr. and Mrs. Richard Kolbe and was born at Hamburg, Germany. When a young boy, he was in charge of the cargoes of the ship of which his father, while in Brazil, died of yellow fever and a year later, while returning from this country, his mother was drowned at the time the "Pomerania" liner sunk.

Surviving are his widow, Mrs. Lillian M. Surbeck Kolbe, a son, Conrad R. Kolbe, a daughter, Miss Helen E. Kolbe, and a grandson, Richard E. Kolbe. The funeral will be held at the home Wednesday afternoon at 2 o'clock. Burial will be at Woodlawn Cemetery.

Figure 3.5 News Article on Gustave A. Kolbe

THOUGHTS OF THE DAY
By Edward H O'Hara
from the SYRACUES HERALD May 30, 1924

How fleeting is memory! Day before yesterday Richard E. Kolbe of the city was borne to his grave. Up in Woodlawn Cemetery today there is being decorated the grave of Gustave A. Kolbe, a brother of Richard E. Kolbe. And while Gustave A. has lain in his grave there for 25 years, no one, in all printed and said of the brother buried last Wednesday has apparently remembered that Gustave A. Kolbe was a member of the 41st Separate Company, National Guard of New York State, and the first soldier killed in the Spanish-American War.

Gustave A. Kolbe was born in Germany and came to America as a sailor. Landing in New Orleans, he soon came to Syracuse where a sister had preceded him. He secured a job with the Whitman and Barnes Manufacturing Company, then of this city, and when it removed to the West he went with it, having meanwhile risen to the foremanship of the works. While here, he was a famed athlete and prominent as a member of the Syracuse Turn Verein.

Almost immediately after he left Syracuse, he enlisted and went to Tampa, Florida, whence he was dispatched to the front, joining the First United States Volunteer Cavalry or Rough Riders. June 24th at La Quasima, he took part in the battle of El Caney, which was the first of the War and the First Cavalry was the first body of troops engaged.

The country where the battle was fought lies in long ridges and upon one of these the First Cavalry was thrown. The thick underbrush and tropical foliate made it an ideal place to resist attack. The Spaniards lay concealed behind trees and bushes and their use of smokeless powder, then a recent invention, made it almost impossible to locate them. Finally Kolbe, catching sight of an enemy through an opening in the trees, fired. The shot uncovered the enemy and the fight was on. It was the first shot, and it spelled death for Kolbe, who fired it. Spanish bullets poured like hail. In a few minutes the gallant and fearless Kolbe fell, pierced by six bullets, the first casualty of the Spanish-American War. In a moment of enthusiasm, he had revealed himself to the enemy.

His brother, now just laid at his side at Woodlawn Cemetery, expressed a desire to have Gustave's body brought home, but was wholly without means to meet the big expense.

The Herald undertook the task and sent its representative, the late Adam C. Haeselbarth, to the War Department at Washington, which consented to undertake the location of the body and to pay transportation charges to Syracuse of the Herald would pay all over costs. Thereupon Mr. Haeselbarth returned to this city and a day or two later, with Undertaker Samuel S. Millin, departed for Santiago, Cuba, where after many perplexities, they located, exhumed and embalmed the body and carried it back to Syracuse.

On Sunday, August 29, 1898, Kolbe was given a public funeral with full military honors, the most imposing ever held in this city.

The Life of John Conrad Surbeck (Grandpa Surbeck)

$\mathcal{J}$ ohn (Johan) Conrad Surbeck was born in 1837 in

Oberhallau in the Canton of Schaffhausen, located near the Lower Rheinfall on the Rheine River, Switzerland. In 1857 he came to Syracuse, New York. A few years later he enlisted during the Civil War with the 2nd New York Cavalry Regiment serving under Generals Sheridan and Custer. He served in the army during the entire war. For part of that time, he was assigned as the bodyguard to General Custer.

Figure 3-6. John Conrad Surbeck

After the Civil War, John Surbeck returned to Syracuse. On March 20th, 1864 he married Margaret Ochsner who was also from Schaffhausen, Switzerland.

Shortly thereafter he acquired a farm and started his feed mill business that became a great financial success. Dealing in four, feed, meal, and grain, his business at 126 and 128 North Warren Street was one of the biggest of its kind in New York State. Along with feed he also sold "Swiss, Limburg, and Green Cheese" as well as "Holland Herring and French Mustard." His farm in the neighborhood of James Street was considered "a model farm in every regard."

John and Margaret had one child, Lillian Marguerite Surbeck, who eventually married Richard Kolbe and gave birth to three children; Conrad Kolbe (the author of these stories), Helen Kolbe (who became Mrs. Vern Botsford and moved to Springfield, N.Y.) and Constance who died as a child about age 12.

The Surbeck's family home was at 404 Highland Street in Syracuse. When daughter Lillian married, she and her husband Richard Kolbe moved nearby, into 402 Highland Street. John Surbeck was 84 when he died of "a lingering illness" in 1932, having survived his son-in-law Richard Kolbe by eight years.

The following page shows a photograph of the 2nd New York Cavalry Regiment taken sometime during the Civil War (1861-1865). In the photo of the regiment, John Surbeck is the 7th standing man from the left. Seated in front of him, with his profile to camera, is General Sheridan. Note that the structure in the photo is a wall tent that has been shot full of holes.

Figure 3-7. The 2nd N.Y. Cavalry, circa 1861-1864.
Seated in profile is General Sheridan, with John Surbeck
standing directly behind the general's hands.

The following poem was written as a eulogy to John Surbeck by award-winning poetess Katherine S. Brown, whose daughter Minabelle Baltzel Brown married John Surbeck's grandson, Conrad Richard Edward Kolbe (Big Dad).

FOR GREATER SYRACUSE

Dedicated to the memory of
John C. Surbeck, an Eastwood Pioneer

by
Katherine S. Brown

A sturdy youth, some three score years or more
With sterling worth, came to Eastwood's door
With labor and skill, he beautified
A country field by the highroad side.
Today home sites his fine efforts have won
For here was laid the foundation of beautiful Arlington.

A suburb, well sought, this Eastwood spot
With wide spreading maples, a building lot.
The fertile soil, where flowers will grow
The rolling land, from which water will flow.
Away from the city's dust and strife
Where pure breath of nature, adds to one's life.

For mountains in homeland far away
A street he named Rigi, one sees today.
Far sighted this man of integrity
Instrumental in Eastwood's prosperity.
Now happily we find he lived to see
This village growing to a great city.

PENUMBRA

Now the old dirt road has passed away
And so this pioneer of yesterday.
The streets and houses built well he planned
Monuments to his efforts now they stand.
Eastwood with a greater city in view
Youth of today she is calling for you.

Large industries have come here to stay
Here there is bus service night and day
The statistics tell us up to date
Was fastest growing village in the state
Churches, schools, business and her progress of today
*   Eastwood for greater Syracuse has paved her way.*

The Poetess Katherine Sarah Bubb Baltzel Brown (Grandma Brown)

by Eunice Kolbe Ross

Katherine Sarah Bubb Baltzel Brown, known to many of us as Grandma Brown, was the mother of Minabelle Kolbe and the mother-in-law of Conrad Richard Kolbe. Grandma Brown was born to a family of seven children -- Elizabeth (Libby), George, Katherine Sarah and Sarah Katherine (twins), Minnie, Isabel (Belle), and Henry. Their mother Philomena was very kind and loving. Of her father, Grandma Brown always said proudly that her father was a "letter carrier." She could remember "thumping" the piano as a little girl. She never had piano lessons but could play lovely advanced music by ear. When I was a child I recall that she sat at the piano playing and smiling widely as I danced around her.

Katherine's father died when the children were very young and she left school to work at a factory at 13 years of age. Although she was not able to finish her high school education, Katherine remained proud. One day a man followed her and her best friend Eliza (for whom she wrote her poem "A Garden of Friendship"). The man made some remarks but the girls carried their heads high and ignored him.

Finally, the man said, "Who do you think you are? You're only shop girls."

Figure 3-8. Katherine Sarah Bubb Baltzel Brown (Grandma Brown) on far right, taken around 1932.

From left: Lillian Surbeck Kolbe (Big Dad's mother, Grandma Kolbe), Carol June Kolbe, Minabelle Kolbe, Eunice Winifred Kolbe, Conrad Richard Kolbe, Jr. (Bud), and Grandma Brown.

Before they walked on, Katherine proudly retorted, "Shop girls, yes. But, oh my!"

Though her formal education was limited, Katherine made good friends and educated herself. She recited poetry for cultural groups including "The Ladies Historical Society." After one such reading, a prominent member of the society congratulated her on her writings and said she had a remarkable vocabulary. Later, Katherine asked me meekly, "Eunny, what does vocabulary mean?"

She entered a nationwide competition to describe Mt. Rushmore at the time it was being carved, and she competed against hundreds of writers in the country, including professional writers and professors. She was awarded third prize.

Her fine young husband Louis Baltzel came from a proud homestead in Lyons, New York. He died of diphtheria from drinking water from a polluted well, leaving Katherine with baby Minabelle to support. Katherine was too plucky to accept charity even in the days of few job opportunities for women, and she became a police matron. Part of the benefits of the job was that she and little Minabelle lived in the City Hall Building of Syracuse. It was there that she met Sergeant David Brown who was to marry her and became the beloved step-father of Minabelle. When Katherine left the force, the policemen gave her a token of their esteem which she valued always.

Katherine was a strong personality and advocated high morals. She was a Christian and her daughter was raised in Westminster Presbyterian Church where she was to meet and marry Conrad Richard Edward Kolbe. It was in this church where their children -- Conrad Richard, Jr. (Bud), Carol, and myself were baptised and raised.

What I remember most about Grandma Brown is how

Figure 3-9. Katherine Sarah Bubb Baltzel Brown
(Grandma Brown).

deeply she loved us grandkids. Conrad, Jr. (Bud, or Sonny Boy), Carol, and I were the apples of her eye. She was extremely proud and devoted to us. We were among the world's greatest children to Grandma. When Carol and I visited her house she might even serve us breakfast in bed and take us special places on the trolly car, and later on the bus. As we grew old enough to date, Grandma became suspicious of the world and overprotective of us but it was because she cared so much about us.

Of the her great-grandchildren, Grandma Brown only got to see Keith and Christine. By then she was living with Minabelle and Conrad, her daughter and son-in-law. When the grand-babies visited Grandma Brown in her room her eyes smiled and radiated the joy she knew in loving them. How she would have enjoyed all her great-grandchildren -- Keith, Christine, Mary, Charles, Lisa, Mandy, Stephanie, and Ed.

In her last days in the hospital (around 1953) she was in great discomfort and was depressed. She moaned continually except when I told her the doings of her two great-grandchildren. Then she smiled broadly with interest. I apologized to the other ladies in her room for talking so much about the children and they said, "Please don't stop. Listening about them is all that stops that moaning."

She loved her family to the end. When I reach Heaven's Shores I will look for Grandma Brown -- up front in the receiving line, smiling her love and welcome.

Grandma always meant to publish her poems. I promised myself one day before the grandchildren were married and gone that I would collect what poems I could and get them copied and in her beloved family's hands.

The siblings of Katherine Sarah Bubb Baltzel Brown included four sisters and two brothers. The oldest sister Elizabeth (Libby) married Foss Peters. Foss got his first name from the doctor who delivered him (Dr. Foss). Foss's mother died when he was very young. His father remarried and Foss was taken in by his step-mother. But when Foss' father died and his step-mother remarried, the new step-father turned him away at age 9. At age 12 Foss got a job driving horses on the Erie Canal, travelling from Syracuse all the way to New York City. Canal men had to be tough and Foss Peters became a boxer and eventually a sparring partner for the well-known boxer John L. Sullivan. Libby and Foss had one son, John Edward Peters who fathered a daughter, Beulah Peters. Sadly, John Edwards Peters did not get to see his daughter grow up because he died at age 21 of tuberculosis. For Libby and Foss, the loss of their son was devastating and Libby never got over it.

Katherine's youngest sister Isabel (Belle) married Mr. Miller. While Belle was pregnant, Mr. Miller fell from the roof of a construction job and was killed before his daughter, Bernice, was born.

After that, Belle had a rather scandalous relationship with a man who proposed, then refused to marry her. Bell took him to court, which was an unusual move at the time as it publicly branded her a bold woman. With her reputation in question, she moved to New York City and eventually married Jacob Samuel Solomon. Known to many of us as Uncle Jake, he was the shop steward for the electrical union and was rather well-known amongst his peers. Figure 3-8 shows a photograph of Jacob taken with the much-loved mayor of New York City, Fiorello La Guardia.

Belle and Jake had no children together. Belle's daughter Bernice from her first marriage ended up marrying a Mr. Couch in New York and became Bernice Miller Couch.

Later in life, Beulah Peters reported that she had been close to her second cousins Bernice and Minabelle. The three girls were close in age and as the fathers of all three had died very young, they all knew what it was like to be fatherless.

Katherine's sister Minnie married Henry Baker. Unfortunately, Minnie was in a car accident with her sister Belle. Belle was driving the car in Syracuse on a hill at the time when the brakes failed. Bell jumped out quickly, before the car was going very fast. Minnie jumped out later, after the vehicle had gained momentum, and was quite injured. She remained in pain for the rest of her life, which was very likely shortened by the accident.

Katherine's twin sister Sarah Katherine (an inversion of her first and middle name) died around five years of age at a baseball game after being struck by a ball. This was before chain link fences were erected at games to protect the audience members from stray balls.

Katherine's two brothers were George and Henry. Henry was the "good" brother who died young as a teenager. George, who was older than Katherine, was the naughty brother who was something of a playboy and a prankster. Once as a young man, his family entertained a German guest. George knew a bit of German, and told his sister some words to properly greet their guest. The poor German man was shocked when she pleasantly told him, "Du bist ein Dumkopf." In other words, *you are a dunce.*

George Bubb had a son, John Bubb, although I can't' find any mention of a wife. George lived a long life and when he was quite old, he moved in with his sister Katherine (Grandma Brown) into her two family house in Syracuse on Oak Street. Perhaps fitting with his carefree playboy life, his last words were, "I'm cashing in my chips."

Figure 3-9. Jacob Solomon (center). To his right is Fiorello La Guardia, the popular mayor of New York City from 1934-1945. At far right is Harry Von Arsdale of New York's Electrical Union Local 3, known as 'Top Hat Harry.' To Jake's left is Mrs. Perkins, the Secretary of Labor.

SECTION 4

The Poetry of Katherine Sarah Bubb Baltzel Brown (Grandma Brown),
mother of Minabelle and mother-in-law of Conrad Richard Edward Kolbe (Big Dad)

A Garden of Friendship

Dedicated to the Memory of my Life Long Friend
Mrs. Elizabeth Edwards

by K. Brown

In childhood we planted a garden

Wherein a real friendship grew
Yesteryear in playtime so dear
With cheeks aglow from childish cheer
We nourished that friendship true.

In youth our garden flourished
For our friendship we'd oft renew
With confidences, smiles and tears
As we passed on through the years
We became staunch pals we two.

In womanhood our garden stood
Beautified a tribute fond and true
Recollections dear to heart and life
Where out of our garden of friendship
A flower was plucked,' twas you.

In sorrow our garden lies withered
While spared I'll make it anew
With memories sweetest token
Though our friendship has been broken

I'll plant it with memories of you.

You and I

by K. Brown

When we two met on life's pathway

Little we thought love had its sway.
But our friendship grew as days passed by
And entered the hearts of you and I.

Kind remembrance of you a part
I'll treasure deeply in my heart
On life's pathway we have our mood
With sunshine, rain, bad days and good.

Love is a gift from God above
May we ever cherish that true love
Divine guidance you and I will ask
As we embark on life's holy task.

A Picture Beautiful

by K. Brown

Far away in the wildwood

Is a place I love to roam
With my books amongst the flowers
Where the bees their honey comb.

While I read the birds are singing
In their sweetest tone to me
It seems an earthly paradise
And I wonder what heaven must be.

For nature has painted her glory
On bird, flower, sprig, and tree
And oh, such wondrous beauty
On canvas one never can see.

Give thanks to the Great Creator
For the world in which we live
If we could but see the beautiful
Our lives would be enriched to give.

Springtime

by K. Brown

Oh, for the breath of nature

Time of the year called Spring
When all mankind and creature
The Creator's praises sing.

Oh for warmth of Spring sunshine
That brings the flowers to bloom
And joy to the heart of a shut-in
As it chases away the gloom.

To hear the sweet notes of the robin
As from tree top again he will sing --
There's no bird we welcome so gladly
As this pretty harbinger of Spring.

To gather early violets peeping through the snow
Or climb the wooded hillside where arbutus grow
To hear the children's voices as outdoors they ring --
Something we'll always cherish, that time called Spring.

Summer Time

by K. Brown

In the beauty of creation

Summer justly follows spring
Adorned with such wondrous beauty
And tree song birds gently sing.

'Tis summer when the roses bloom
Their sweet fragrance scenting the air,
And nature has painted her glory
In every hue everywhere.

Oh, for the joy of the summer
That brings to hearts comfort and cheer
Basking in warmth of God's sunshine
Or dip in waters cool and clear.

Give thanks to The Great Creator
For the summer's sunrise at morn
Sunset's glorified at twilight
And nature whose beauties adorn.

'Tis Autumn

by K. Brown

The winds are sighing through the trees

Branches are shaken by the breeze
When the winds grow bolder
Then the days grow colder
      'Tis Autumn.

When leaves are tinted red and gold
Wondrous beauty we then behold
But now they are falling
All nature is calling
      'Tis Autumn.

In gratitude for ingathered grain
The reapers song we hear again
When the harvest moon is shining
Round firesides we're reclining
      'Tis Autumn.

When the harvest days are ended
God's harvest with praise we behold
When the frost has touched the pumpkin
And the foliage turned to gold,
      'Tis Autumn.

Winter

by K. Brown

Winter comes in her serene majesty

Robed in a blanket of pure white snow
We stand and gaze at this celestial sight
While snow flakes playfully fall to and fro

They fall to the earth without a sound
Like a soft carpet they cover the ground
On a cold frosty night with heavenly light
They sparkle like diamonds in the night.

On life's pathway the seasons have their moods
With sunshine, rain and snow all for our good.
When bitter cold wintry winds blow and blast
Her crystal house trim is holding fast.

Each season has its splendor true
Like love's old story ever new,
Springtime the violets, summer, the rose.
Autumn golden leaves and winter the snows.

A Birthday Greeting to President Franklin D. Roosevelt

by K. Brown

United we stand throughout this great land,

Regardless of factions, hand in hand.
All Americans we can proudly say
As we glorify our President's natal day.

Helping those afflicted on life's pathway
To Franklin D. Roosevelt tribute we pay
Through his achievement our nation stands
With loving hearts and ever ready hands.

For thee, dear President, we trust and pray,
That God will guide and bless you day by day
With increased wisdom and power we ask
To sustain you in your difficult task.

With cheer from loyal hearts we wish you this day,
A Happy Birthday and many on the way
To our leader who over prejudice will tower
We greet you, President Roosevelt,
        The Man of the Hour!

Sweet Songs of Yore -

Dedicated to the Memory of
George M. Cohen

by K. Brown

The sweetest songs are those of yore

We love to sing them O'er and or'e.
New songs come, some stay some go
How or when we will never know.

George M. Cohen kindled a flame
In hears of old with sweet refrain
As they sang with him Sweet and Low,
Loves Old Sweet Songs, on radio.

When You and I were Young, Maggie,
Alice Benbolt, Annie Laurie,
The Sweetest Story Ever Told
Silver Threads Amongst the Gold.

Swing time, Blues, love songs and what
Big Apple, Jazz and Turkey Trot
All have their day as years toll by
But sweet songs of yore never die.

A Tribute to Syrico Seniors

by K. Brown

On the hills of Onondaga

When the skies were azure blue
A pleasure we'll all remember
When we climbed the slopes with you.

After four long years of study
"God's" wide world is waiting for you
Cultured, fame and all glory too
S.U. seniors, as we bid them adieu.

The Auto Digested

by K. Brown

The automobile puts on airs

with H20, oil, gas, and repairs
Old or new, tin pan or plate
She is advertised up to date.

She'll carry you on high or low
It matters not the distance
The auto is of man a part
It is Woman's new existence.

A Want Ad

by K. Brown

If you want roofs, clothes, autos, or carts

Pairs or repairs, cures, crafts or arts
Lots, houses, flats, room warm or cold
male or female, lost found, or sold
The wealth of your attic turned into gold.

SECTION 5

The House of Conrad Richard Kolbe and Minabelle Baltzel Brown Kolbe at 3412 James Street, Syracuse

The History of the House at 3412 James Street, Syracuse

Figure 5-1. 3412 James St., Syracuse.
From a Syracuse Post Card

The brick Colonial house at 3412 James Street in the Eastwood district of Syracuse, New York, was a wedding present to Conrad and Minabelle Kolbe who were married in 1918. The land and the building costs were paid by Conrad's maternal grandfather, John C. Surbeck. John Surbeck owned quite a bit of land in Eastwood and young Conrad often accompanied his grandfather Surbeck as he travelled in his horse and buggy to collect rent in the area. John Surbeck donated the land for Eastwood's Methodist Church and named Rigi Ave after the Rigi Mountains of Switzerland where he was born.

Sometime around 1918, Minabelle chose her house plans from "The House Beautiful" magazine. The magazine article that caught her attention is shown in figure A-1.

Apparently, Minabelle altered the plans somewhat and reversed the porch wing and the kitchen wing.

The floor plans from the original blueprints of the house, designed to meet Minabelle's exacting specifications by architect Edward A. Howard, are shown in figure A-2.

While the house was being built, Conrad and Minabelle lived with her mother, Mrs. Katherine S. Brown. When the house was completed, the newlyweds moved in and lived there for the next 50 years until the death of Minabelle in 1969.

At one time, the house was prominently featured in advertisements for the McCain Realty Company which sold lots in the Eastwood area. One of these advertisements is shown in figure A-3. Arlington, the name proposed in these advertisements for the upper James Street area, apparently never caught on.

Figure 5-2. Big Dad's house at 3412 James St., Syracuse

Another time, the house graced the front of Syracuse postcards. The picture of the house on page 104 was taken from such a post card. I understand that the house has also been discussed in a 1980's Syracuse University publication on older homes in the Syracuse area.

The lovely brick house with its graceful white pillars still stands today, as stately and regal as ever, at 3412 James Street.

Figure 5-3. The 1918 article from *THE HOUSE BEAUTIFUL* magazine that caught Minabelle's attention.

ARE YOU PLANNING TO BUILD A HOUSE?

WE ARE BUILDING THIS ONE AND TELLING
ABOUT IT IN THE HOUSE BEAUTIFUL

We selected our land at No. 1662 Commonwealth Avenue, Newton, Massachusetts—one of the prettiest suburbs of Boston—and there we are building this first of a series of HOUSE BEAUTIFUL HOMES—a nine-room structure in the New England Colonial style. The above picture shows something of its charm and attractiveness and the head photographer on our staff has been assigned the duty of showing our readers each step that is taken in building furnishing and equipping of this home.

In the magazine each month we are printing a detailed story of the progress made. We are telling all the difficulties encountered and all the successes achieved. We are telling the whole story from the choosing of the site and the digging of the cellar to that happy day when the house shall stand finished, fully furnished, with grounds and garden completed.

At the present time you may be delaying building the house you are longing to build because you have heard so much about the high cost of construction in these "war times." Well, we are going to tell you item by item what our house costs us—cement for the cellar, bricks for the chimney, shingles for the roof, flooring, doors and plumbing.

We will tell, when the time comes why we choose each particular piece of furniture that goes into the house, and show the position in which it is placed. The color schemes of the rooms will be analyzed. The principles under which the garden is laid out will be explained.

In short, the building, furnishing and arrangement of the house and grounds are planned to serve as an actual, practical guide to those of our readers who plan to build their own homes now or in the near future, or to those who wish to learn new ways of handling old possessions to better advantage.

Some one has said that, after a man has built one house, he wants to build a second one to correct the faults in the first. We intend HOUSE BEAUTIFUL HOMES No. 1 to be our readers' *first house*, so that after watching *our* progress from month to month, their own plans and desires will be so clarified that when *their* house is finished they would not want one item changed.

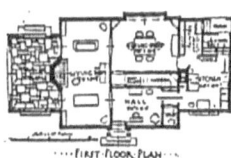

······FIRST-FLOOR PLAN·····

This practical assistance is only one of the things we mean when we talk of the HOUSE BEAUTIFUL service that goes to subscribers for the magazine.

····· SECOND FLOOR PLAN ·····

Complete working plans of HOUSE BEAUTIFUL HOMES NO. 1 are now for sale at a moderate price by THE HOUSE BEAUTIFUL, 3 Park Street, Boston, Mass.

Figure 5-4a. Blueprints for 3412 James Street, Syracuse. Front Elevation.

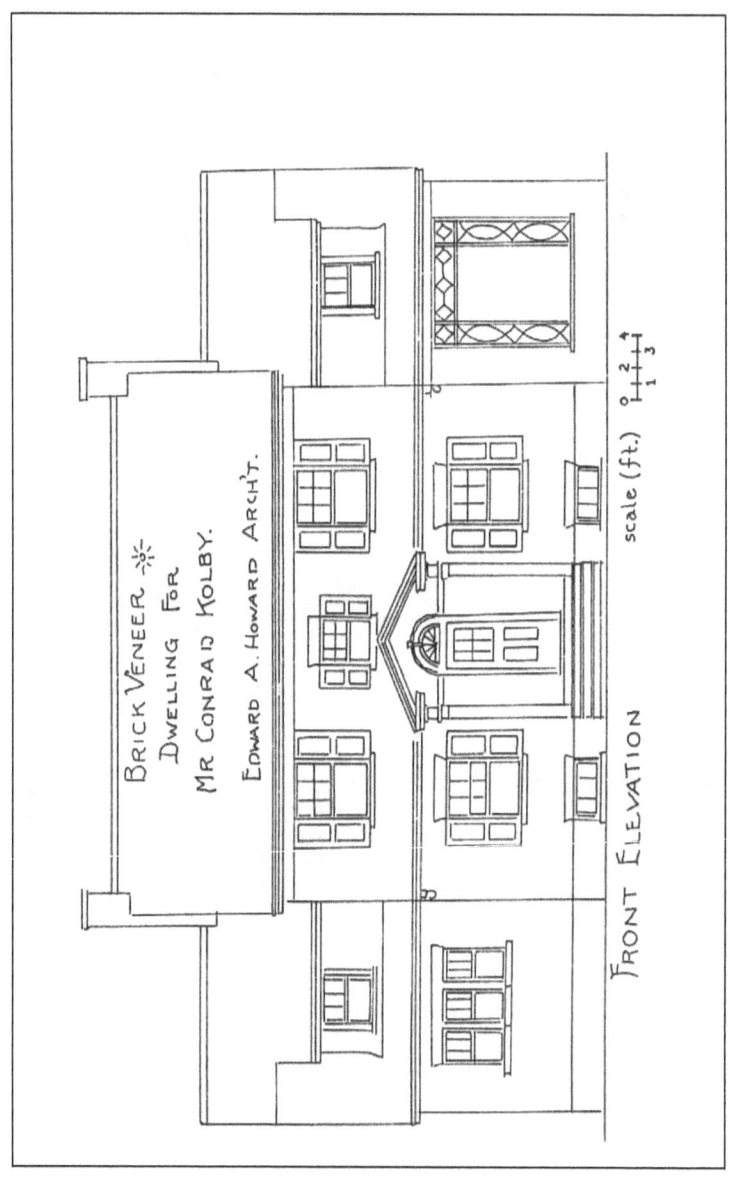

Figure 5-4b. Side Elevation.

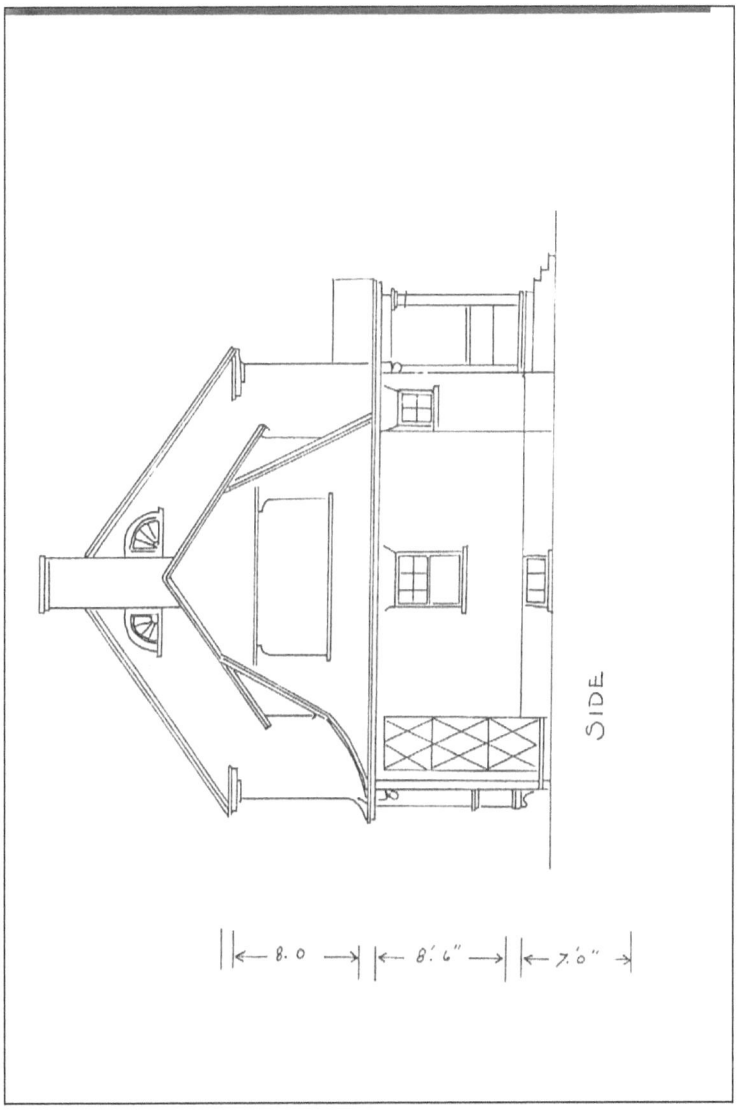

Figure 5-4c. First Floor.

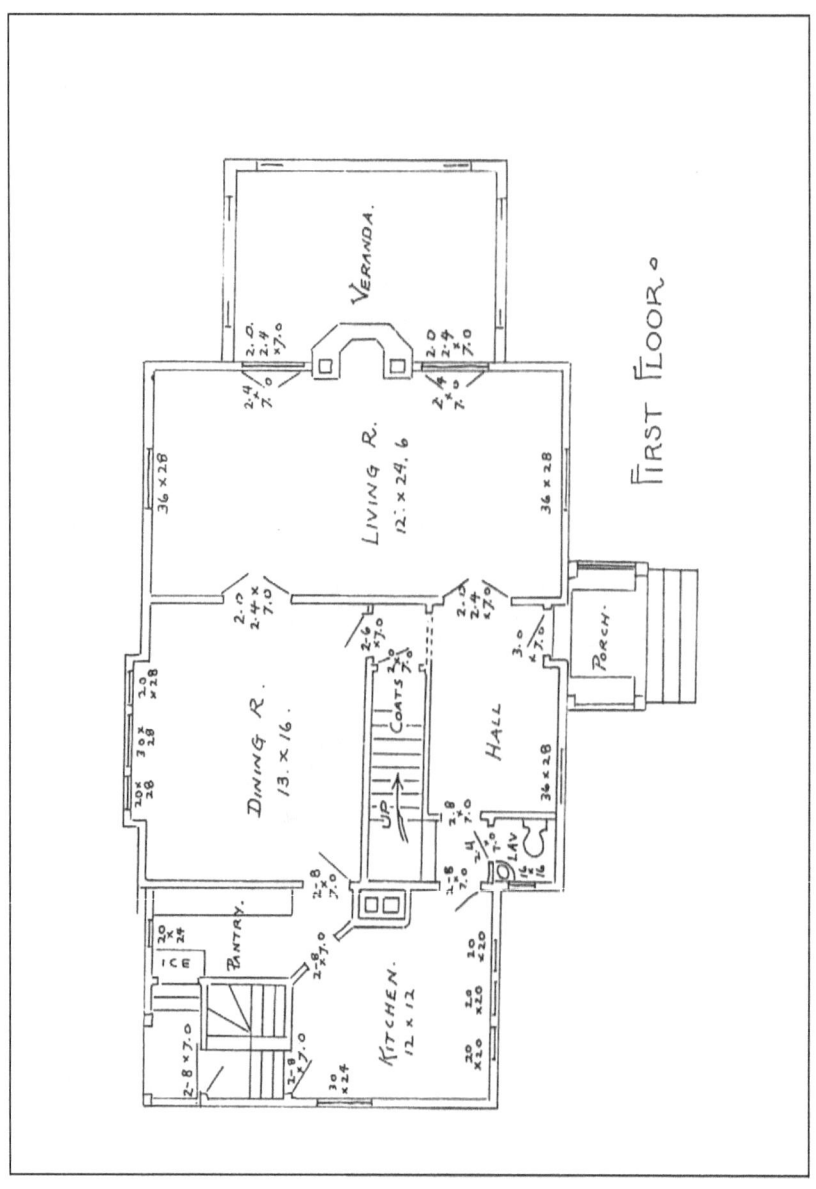

Figure 5-4d. Second Floor.

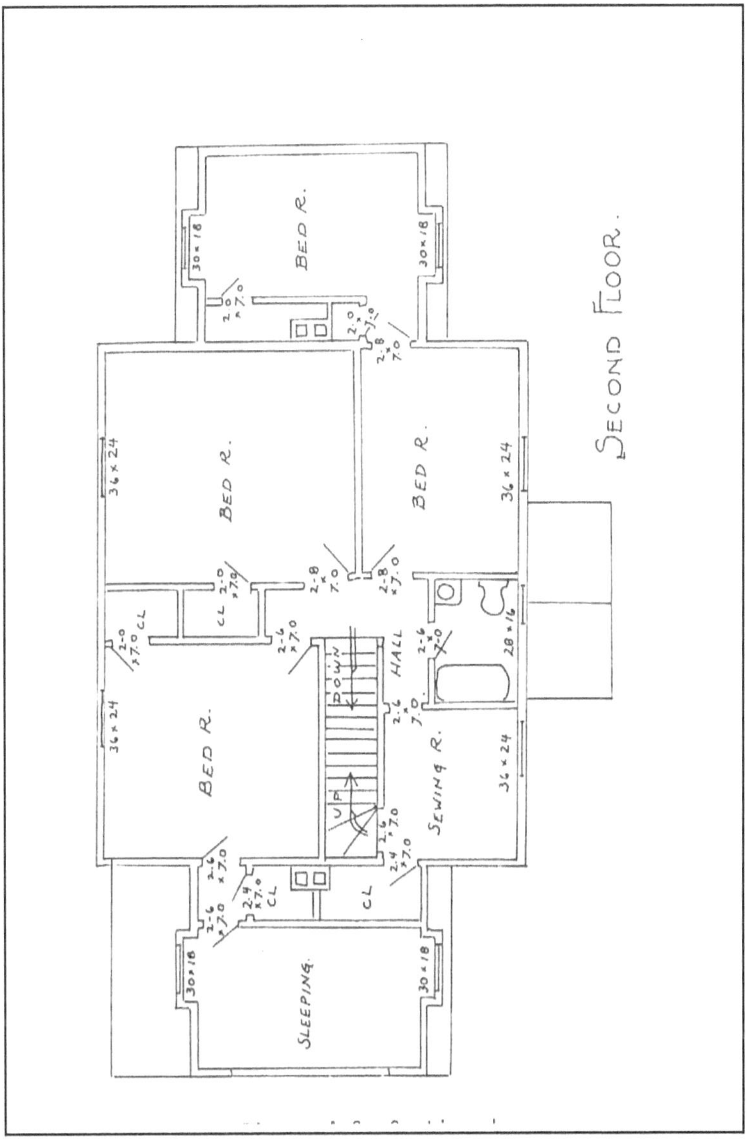

Figure 5-4e. Foundation.

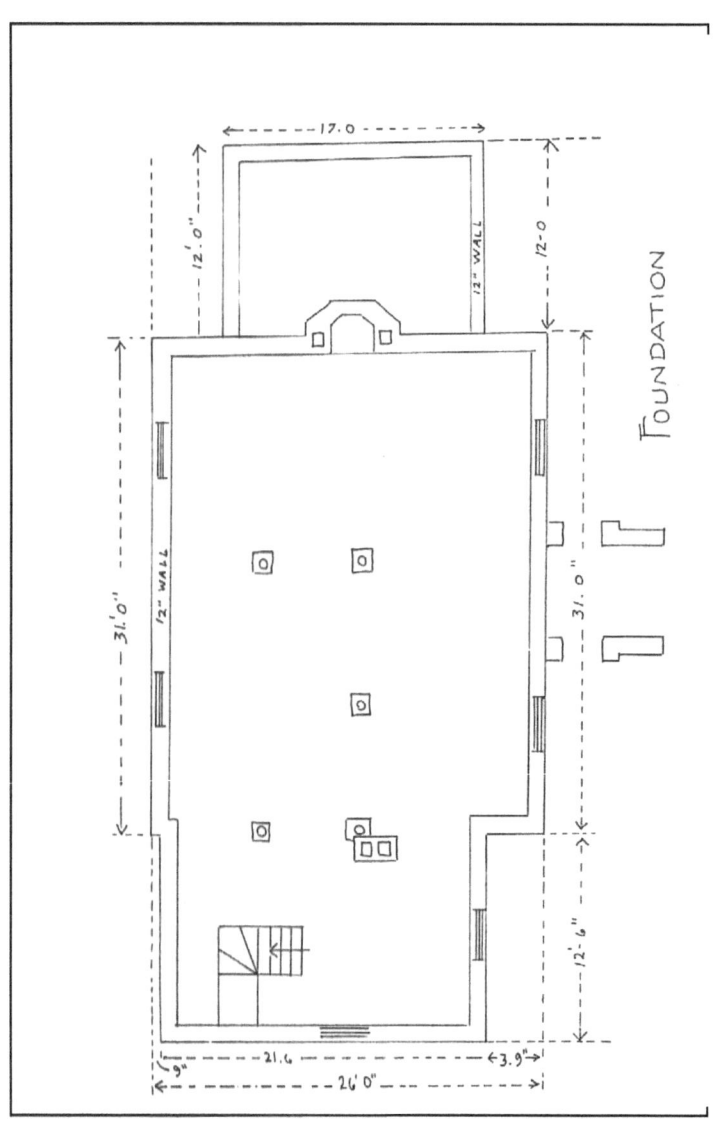

Figure 5-5. Advertisement for "Arlington."

Figure 5-5. Continued.

Figure 5-5. Continued.

Figure 5-5. Continued.

Those who build their homes at ARLINGTON will have every modern living convenience.

Here are two of the James Street Homes at ARLINGTON.

Figure 5-5. Continued.

SECTION 6

Conrad Richard Kolbe, Jr. (Uncle Bud)

Conrad Richard Kolbe, Jr.

It seems that Conrad passed along the writing bug to his son, Conrad Richard Kolbe, Jr. (Uncle Bud), who wrote an account (unpublished) of his war experiences in World War II which he titled 42023909, which was his army serial number.

In his account, Uncle Bud explains how he was assigned to "K" company in the 232nd infantry in the 42nd Rainbow Division. However, he ended up being loaned to "I" company as there were only forty four men left out of the original two hundred eighteen, so they needed more men to help fill the ranks. When he joined "I" company, he was assigned to be first scout and in the battle at the Bulge and he found himself fighting his way through Germany, being "shot at by about every weapon in the Nazi arsenal, pinned down for hours by machine gun nests."

When the movie "Private Ryan" came out, Uncle Bud told me that it was a very realistic depiction of the D Day battle, except for one thing. Apparently, the first wave of soldiers sent in were not only equipped with their weapons but each one also carried a sheet. This was to be used as their personal body bag since they weren't expected to survive. As predicted, a staggering amount did not.

Uncle Bud survived the battle. Later in the war he was sent to Munich to Hitler's residence with orders to assassinate Hitler. He arrived at the residence with some other G.I.'s to find Hitler had already gone and the place "ankle deep" in tea

Figure 6-1. Conrad Richard Kolbe, Jr. (Uncle Bud). Photo taken at the close of WW II in Munich by international photographer Berta Himmler. Miss Himmler was the only photographer ever to photograph Johann Straus and this was after his death as he would refuse to have his image taken on film while he was alive.

bags. Uncle Bud came out of Hitler's residence with a set of sterling silver spoons and a number of bottles of wine, which he promptly drank.

After returning from the war, Uncle Bud kept the spoons although his father, Conrad Sr. (who wrote the short stories in this volume), refused to eat from Hitler's utensils. Uncle Bud ended up taking them up to his vacation house on

Lake Ontario and using them as camp spoons. Being solid silver, they are excellent conductors of heat, and Uncle Bud told me they often got uncomfortably hot and could burn you if used in hot food.

Over the years, most of Hitler's spoons in this set were lost through attrition. Today, only one of those spoons liberated from Hitler's house remains (Figure 6-2).

When I first printed the earlier version of this book for members of the family back in 1988 and sent Uncle Bud a copy, he told me it was "the nicest package of my life" and that he felt that Big Dad "would have been happy to see it." As I put together this current edition and have included some additional material, I thought that Uncle Bud might have appreciated having a few of his works included in this current volume. With that in mind, I have included three of Uncle Bud's moving poems, written during his military service in the war.

Figure 6-2. Hitler's Spoon. This is the last remaining spoon from the set that Uncle Bud liberated from Hitler's Munich residence towards the end of World War II.

D DAY
by Conrad Richard Kolbe, Jr.

The air is taut with ominous meaning,
The sun is hid by fleecious screening,
Hearts of nations beating fast,
Invasion day is here at last.

Ten thousand air craft fill the sky,
A million soldiers stranding by,
Muscles taut with nervous strain,
Lorraine is on the march again.

As brave men fall this terrible day,
Millions bow their heads to pray.
Men's hopes are confirmed this hour,
As Nazis feel full Allied power.

"Oh God may they not die in vain,
Let now ruination rule again."
Let's pray and make our beachheads fast,
Invasion day is here at last.

HEAVY IN HEART

by Conrad Richard Kolbe, Jr.

When the heart is heavy the spirit is weak,
The mind is weary, the lips don't speak.
Sick to the soul, sick as hell,
Sick with the curse of the war-lord's spell.

I'm sick of seeing these men pass by,
Minus a leg, an arm or an eye.
I'm sick of the bombs that come by night
And seeing the people flee in fright.

Sick of all this and wondering why
Millions of innocent people die.
I'm sick of being away from you
Loving you the way I do.

But then we'd be sicker still
If we paid the tyrant's bill.

G. I. JOE

by Conrad Richard Kolbe, Jr.

Sloshing in mud, trudging through snow,
That's tired, wearily, fighting G.I. Joe.
The blisters on feet, the ache of his back
Pictures of loved ones in discarded pack.

The gun in the hands of a peace loving man,
The wind beaten face so bearded and tan.
A moment of rest in the drizzling rain,
Only a moment, then push on again.

Forgot is the month, the hour and the day,
No paper to read, no people to say.
The whine of the bullet, the shock of the shell
Surely it couldn't be much worse in hell.

Over the hills and through ice cold streams,
Nightmarish sights from the wildest of dreams.
The bodies of beasts, women and men
Beginning the turn to dust again.

A can of cold hash, a piece of dried bread,
With crossed bandoleers heavy with lead.
The memories of home, a feeling of pain,
Would he ever see his loved ones again?

Will the world forget these men of fame,
Even though unheard their name,
And through a few years to come
Forget the war so painfully won?

SECTION 7

KOLBES IN HISTORY

Kolbes in History

There are a few historic figures with the Kolbe name.

Saint Maximilian Maria Kolbe, born on January 8th, 1894 was a Polish Franciscan friar. On August 14, 1941 he volunteered to die in place of a stranger (a father with children) in the Nazi German concentration camp of Auschwitz, located in German-occupied Poland during World War II. Forty-one years after his death he was canonized. On October 10th, 1982 Pope John Paul II declared him a martyr of charity and "The Patron Saint of Our Difficult Century."

Figure 7-1. Maximilian Maria Kolbe

Figure 7-2. Statue of Saint Maximilian Maria Kolbe at Westminster Abbey in London, England.

Going back further in time, another famous Kolbe was the chemist Adolph Wilhelm Hermann Kolbe who went by the name **Hermann Kolbe** (1818-1884). He was a German scientist credited with being the first to synthesize an organic compound from an inorganic compound. He also developed the *Kolbe Electrolysis* and *The Kolbe Synthesis* which prepared salicylic acid, a building block of aspirin.

Later in his career, around 1874, Hermann Kolbe's disagreements with other structural chemists of the day began to take on such a critical tone that his writings started to damage his reputation. He died in Germany at the age of 66 from a heart attack in the Saxony town of Leipzig.

Figure 7-3. Herman Kolbe, 1818 - 1884.

Prior to the late 1700s, our Kolbe sir name had been spelled "von Kolbe." At some point, the "von" went out of fashion and was subsequently removed from the name.

During the middle ages when few people besides the village recorder could read or write, von Kolbe was sometimes written down as "von Kalbe" when documenting a birth, and the two names were somewhat interchangeable.

Between 1505-1518 a German physician named **Ulrich** Rühlein **von Kalbe** wrote the first text on mining, EIN NÜTZLICH BERGBÜCHLEIN (a *useful little mountain book*). Writing from his hometown of Freiberg, he penned his work under the pseudonym "Kalbus." Parts of this text were later quoted in Agricola's mining treatise "*De Re Matalica*" published in 1556, which is often but incorrectly considered the first printed book on mining. Von Kalbe's historic text was eventually reproduced and translated into English by the American Institute of Mining Engineers in 1949. Herbert Hoover, a mining engineer, confirmed "bibliophile," and eventually the 31st president of the United States was so impressed with von Kalbe's historic work that he incorporated a woodcut image from it into his personal bookplate used in his library. This library is now a public facility, The Herbert Hoover Presidential Library.

In 1523 at the age of 56 Ulrich von Kalbe died in Germany, also in the Saxony town of Leipzig.

Figure 7-4. The world's first book on mining,
by Ulrich von Kalbe.

PENUMBRA

Big Dad and Minabelle on the tennis court, circa 1920.

www.ingramcontent.com/pod-product-compliance
Lightning Source LLC
Chambersburg PA
CBHW030623130626
46552CB00002B/690